THE UNTOLD STORY

OF THE DARKEST DAYS

Eric Suddoth

Rising Smoke Publishing

Some characters and events in this book are fictious.

Copyright © 2021 Eric Suddoth

Unless otherwise indicated, Scripture quotations are from:
The Holy Bible, English Standard Version copyright © 2001 by Crossway, a publishing ministry of Good News Publishers.
Used by permission. All rights reserved worldwide.

Rising Smoke Publishing
ISBN 978-1-949869-17-0

This book is a work of fiction.

Very little is known about these missing days in history. I sometimes wonder why no one accounted for these days in the Gospels. But my theory is no one wanted to recall their emotions and feelings during these few days when hope was gone.

This is purely my opinion of what the people during this time could have been thinking.

May you read this book with an open mind and heart. May God show you what made these days the darkest days in history.

"When Jesus had received the sour wine,
He said, 'It is finished,'
and He bowed His head and gave up His spirit."

John 19:30, English Standard Version

Chapter 1

Longinus – The Roman Soldier

The ground shook, causing my own legs to become weak. I wasn't used to experiencing a quake this ferocious. I quickly darted my eyes from the top of the hill of Golgotha where I stood guard and looked down onto the city of Jerusalem below and watched the chaos stirring. I saw families running with little hands wrapped tightly, pulling the children behind as their tiny feet dragged the dusty streets causing a cloud of dust to follow.

I thought of my own family. *I hope Helena is safe*, I thought as I surveyed the city and saw that all the buildings seemed intact. I shook my head to stop the faint ringing in my ears, thinking that the shock of the earthquake caused an internal bell to go off inside my head. But it wasn't in my ears; it was coming from somewhere in the town.

Suddenly, the mob that had come to witness the execution of the three criminals scattered when they felt the climatic change. Before the watchers fled, they spit and cursed the dying a few more times for good measure, just to let the sufferers know that death was imminent. I could hear their laughing and crude jokes at the expense of the three naked men who hung with their arms spread wide and their wrists and feet pierced by iron stakes into two splintered wood beams. I glanced up at their hideously exposed and bloody bones that only hours ago were hidden by thick layers of skin and muscle. I saw the looks on their faces. The looks that begged for mercy to end their suffering once and for all.

I was used to the sight of death. I never said that I liked the smell that came when fresh blood was poured out of veins, but I'd learned to live with it. In my line of work, I would rather be the inflictor than the inflicted. I was taught from a young age that men fought, so that is what I did. I fought beside my friends and brothers and watched many of them die at my feet in combat. I tried not to think too much of the times when I had to step over my comrades on the battlefield as they were crying, seconds from death. A few times someone would reach out their hands, catching my foot, but I never looked back. Looking back meant taking my eyes off my enemies. Many times the matter of life and death came down to split seconds. I never told my mother that I kicked my brother in the face to get him to release his grip. He was going to die anyway, but I wasn't going to let his death bring about my own. I just wasn't.

I was taught early on to stifle any emotions or sympathy. These were criminals that deserved to die. These were murderers who, if not killed, might kill someone I knew and loved, like my wife, Helena. If it ever came between killing them or letting them kill her, I would do anything to keep her safe. Anything. I might have been just a solider in Jerusalem far from battle, but there was a warrior under my uniform. A warrior ready and willing to fight for Rome.

The sunlight that had been blinding just a few minutes ago quickly faded behind a thick swarm of storm clouds. I saw my commander, Maximus, running up the hill, pushing through the fleeing crowds as a streak of lightning flashed across the blackening sky.

"Break 'em!" he ordered as Classius and I grabbed our wooden weapon of choice. He slammed the bat onto one of the criminal's legs, Dismas, from what I remembered hearing people chant.

"No, no, no!" Gestas, the criminal hanging above me, moaned with bloody tears as he saw me coming in his direction. I had a duty to obey Governor Pilate's orders. I gripped the smooth wood with both my hands and reared my arms and shoulders back. I tuned out his whimpering and caught sight of his trembling toes. I looked up past the bloody stake and ankle and aimed at his shins. His legs were twisted one on top of the other, so I knew I would break at least one on the first swing, if not both.

I swung my arms and felt the bat connect with his bones, breaking them instantly. His body fell without the strength in his legs to hold himself up. His crying stopped. Gasping and gagging was the only thing escaping through his chapped and sunburned lips.

"Want to do the honors to the King of the Jews? Where's your God now?" Classius asked sarcastically, as he bowed on one knee to the lifeless man.

"I will," I said as I stomped away from the suffocating Gestas and swung my bat around to flick off some of his blood. I raised my elbows and took aim at his frozen legs. I had never had remorse for doing my job before, but something about doing this act to this man just didn't seem right. There was something I couldn't put my finger on, but I had a job to do and I always did my job. I planted my feet for a firm stance and took a deep breath.

"Stop!" Maximus shouted. I stopped in mid-swing, looking back at my commander in confusion. "Looks like he's already dead."

"I'll check," I said, throwing down my bat and grabbing my spear that I had leaned against Gestas' cross. I lifted up the sharp metal tip and pierced the side of the lifeless man. He didn't flinch. He didn't moan. He didn't make any sound or movement.

I stood under his lifeless body and waited for the blood to gush, but something was different. As I stood, I watched blood and water spill from his side. I had performed many executions before, but this was the first time water poured from someone's side.

I stood under the shower and something changed inside me. I could not explain it. It was as if the water had some mystical power. I heard Classius say something, but I was too mesmerized to look away. Something was beckoning me to stay. To be cleansed.

For the first time, I felt like I was all alone, yet I felt surrounded by some unknown force. I felt like this man I was staring at, this dead man, was looking directly at me. As if he knew me. My senses faded. I couldn't see anything but this supposed King of the Jews. The world around me seemed to be going in chaos, swirling around at an incredible speed, yet I felt in peace. I glanced over and saw Classius yelling something at me, but I couldn't hear him. All I could hear were faint sounds of some women crying.

I turned around and found a group of women huddled together as one man held tightly to the woman in the center. I didn't know who they were, but I knew they were there for this man. I didn't know this man, but something in my gut was telling me something was wrong here. This man didn't belong here. It was as if all my years of training vanished. I was taught to do my job without sympathy and emotion, yet a strange feeling was coming over me.

4

"Certainly this man was innocent," I mumbled under my breath looking at the band of grievers and then back at the lonely man on the cross.

Classius walked over to me. "You alright?"

I looked at him bewildered. I didn't know if I was alright. I couldn't answer that question because I didn't know what alright meant anymore. I just nodded my head as he walked back to Maximus.

"As soon as they are dead, we have to get them down fast," I heard Maximus say. "Looks like it's about to storm."

I looked up at the sky and had a hard time seeing anything. The sun had vanished and only a vastness of black remained. I looked around the ground for a lantern, but who would have thought we would have needed one just fifteen minutes ago? Even if I did have one, I didn't have any fire to light it with on this hill. A rain drop hit my bare arm. Then another and another.

I glanced over at Maximus and Classius who were looking around, trying to figure out what to do next.

Suddenly I felt a tap on my shoulder. I whipped around startled as an older man stood face to face with me. His eyes were somber and had a look of defeat in the hazel coloring.

"I have permission from Pilate to take this man's body," the man solemnly said pointing up at the King of the Jews. He couldn't look at the deceased man. I didn't know this man who was speaking to me, but he clearly felt there was something different about the supposed King of the Jews.

I looked up at the dead man and another strange feeling coursed through me.

I knew I wanted to know more about this man.

This man named Jesus.

Chapter 2

Joseph of Arimathea

"I have permission from Pilate to take this man's body," I said sadly. I couldn't bear to look up at Jesus. I felt ashamed for sneaking away during the crucifixion to ask Pilate for Jesus' body so no one would see me. My friend was being executed like a thief by some of my other friends on the council. If the council found out my plans for Jesus, they would have surely sought me out. They would have called me a traitor and stripped me of my position, and my position was my livelihood.

My insides were sore from the crushing blows of guilt and remorse as I did nothing to stop his death. I should have said something in the last week to stop all of the manipulation and scheming. The council had been talking for a while of revengeful ways of knocking this man down, but I had thought it was all talk.

At first I would listen to them and pose questions like, "Really, what has this man done?"

But after a few snide remarks from the other members of the council, I started to keep my opinions to myself. I started to live a double life. I wanted to learn more of this prophet that the council was warning me against; in fact, the more they warned, the more I became intrigued.

"He is going to destroy the sanctity of the temple," I remember one man boasting as the other men nodded in agreement. "He is performing acts that only Lucifer himself could do, so he must be possessed. He just must!"

I remember being in the inner circle of the council, and it was always so easy to get caught up in the commotion. Every young man revered and looked up to these holy men, and deep down inside every young man wanted to become them one day. I, too, fell victim to the notoriety that these religious men possessed. They had the power and prestige that gave them the entitlement to say and do whatever they wanted. That need for recognition lured me into their circle. I soon became a yes-man, agreeing with everything that the high priest said. Even if it didn't sound right, I never spoke up because he was the high priest. Who was I to rebut him and his company?

Soon I rose up in the ranks, attended the weekly meetings, had some say in disputes, and gave my opinion in religious ceremonies. I had a voice and it felt unbelievable. I didn't have the final say, but still, I was getting there. I got caught up in the power.

There were a few of us that felt uneasy with the council's responses in the last few years. We were starting to see some of the men on the council felt they had the holy power of God to condemn at the blink of an eye. And they used their power to get what they wanted: more power.

It took a while for me to wake up from the pungent group of people I was surrounding myself with. But even when I started to see through their veils of corruption, I did little to stop it.

When the council was complaining of Jesus' theatrics, I couldn't take their word anymore. I had to see for myself what the issue was. I had to see some of the so-called miracles that always seemed to be around him.

One afternoon I followed a large crowd and found Jesus teaching. His teaching was very sound. I couldn't rebuke anything he was saying. I looked around the crowd and noticed that people from all ages and backgrounds would stop what they were doing to listen to him. He spoke with authority and power, yet he had a way to share it with love and mercy. He spoke of loving one's neighbors, even the people we had always been told to hate. I found his teaching uplifting, but at the same time, his words would cut me deeper than anyone could. I didn't want to live as a hypocrite, and the words he was saying made me the very definition of one. But instead of blasting me, he pointed me to a new direction. My heart felt free.

If it wasn't enough to be fed spiritually, he somehow took some people's leftovers and formed a feast that fed thousands. I remained baffled by that afternoon even though I saw it with my own two eyes. As I listened and watched, I knew this man wasn't possessed like the council was saying. No, he was someone to follow, not condemn.

"Him?" the Roman centurion asked, pointing up at Jesus.

All I could do was nod. I couldn't even look up. I didn't want to see his face, such a sincere and innocent face, looking beaten and tattered. I couldn't look up. I just couldn't.

The Roman soldier got one of his other comrades to help take Jesus' body down off of the cross. I stood numb. I lifted my eyes up and saw the stakes piercing his calloused red feet stained with his blood. My stomach dropped at the thought of the pain of being nailed through the tendons of my feet and to support myself on a rusty nail. I looked around for a place to throw up and caught the eyes of Mary, his mother, looking up at me.

9

My eyes filled with tears as I looked down at a friend who was beside herself in pain and agony. I couldn't imagine what she was going through, seeing her pride and joy hanging on a criminal's cross after being tortured within an inch of his life with the cat o' nine tails. She quickly turned her head, looked above, and gasped in horror. She let out a heart-wrenching wail, and I couldn't stand to look at her anymore. I quickly turned around, instinctively looking up.

Jesus' body was starting to fall forward as each of the guards had removed the nails from his spread arms. I watched in shame as my friend was hurling toward the ground. I couldn't let him be treated like this. I stepped forward as his crimson-covered body fell into my arms, and his feet slid off the lonely nail.

I flinched in pain when his head fell onto my bicep, as the humiliating crown of thorns pierced my skin. One measly thorn, and I flinched.

I looked down at his face, but he didn't look like my friend from two days ago. His tender smile that had radiated joy was swollen and split from punches by the guards. His eyes that had drawn people in with honesty and compassion were bruised shut. His long brown locks were now dripping with blood and tangled with the mocking crown as its thorns sunk deep into his skin.

My lips started to quiver as I looked down his torso and saw rips in his flesh. This carpenter had muscles to build anything out of wood, and the Roman guards had torn off his rippling stature until only fragments remained in a bloodbath of tyranny.

I leaned down and tried to whisper an apology in his ear, but I couldn't get the words out. I was afraid that if I opened my mouth, anything that I had left inside would come out. I continued to cling to his body as the rain started to fall harder smearing the dried blood on his face.

The rain started to wash away some of the filth, showing a clearer image of the pain he'd endured. As the rain pelted my head, I felt safe to shed my tears. If anyone saw me, they would think it was just rain trickling down my cheeks, not my guilt-ridden tears.

"I'm so sorry," I tried to mouth once again, but the words still would not come. I held his body against my chest as my feet were frozen to the ground. I knew I needed to take him to his final resting place, but I knew that the first step I took would finalize my questions. I felt as though if I could just stand still and pretend like this didn't happen, then it didn't. If I could just stand in the rain for the rest of my life, then this would be just a dream I would wake up from. It was as if I could remove all my regret for not shouting, "Crucify Barabbas!"

I had stood motionless as the crowd roared for Jesus to be crucified in place of a known murderer. I stood motionless again.

I looked down one more time and felt my soul tighten as I examined the woven crown of thorns and noticed that one of the thorns had barely missed his eye. "I'm sor-," I started to say when I heard a familiar voice behind me.

"Let me help you, Joseph."

Chapter 3
Nicodemus

"Let me help you, Joseph," I said, barely making it up the hill in time to help him carry Jesus. I could see by the expression on his face he was crumbling, just like we all were.

I laid down some clean linens on the ground and grabbed Jesus' legs to help Joseph gently place him on the ground. My heart stopped for a second as my hand grazed over the wound on his foot where the nails had been a minute ago.

A few of the women started to follow me when they saw me walking up the hill, but I asked them to stay behind. I didn't want them to see him up close before we could clean him up a little better, even though they already knew what he was going to look like.

"How…" Joseph started to ask me, and I knew exactly what he was going to say.

How did this happen? How could anyone want to kill this man who healed the sick, raised the dead, and fed the thousands? How could anyone want to do this to a man so beyond anyone else on this planet? He exuded love to the scoundrels on the street when many people would just pass them without regard. He gave attention to the forgotten when many people turned a blind eye to their disabilities and afflictions. He gave a name to the orphaned and a reason for living to the hopeless.

I knelt beside Joseph and felt what he was feeling. We were in the same social circle of the religious zealots. Yes, I was a Pharisee by outward appearance, but inwardly I was someone else.

I understood the ramifications we were placing ourselves in by helping our friend, Mary, with Jesus' burial. But if anything happened, I would make an excuse. I'd had years of being in the council and my history would speak for itself. Only a few knew I spoke to Jesus about his teachings because I would only seek him in secret. And if anyone said otherwise, I would just deny it.

Part of me wondered if maybe he was a fraud. Maybe the council was right about him. The last two days had spun out of control, and I was lost hanging onto a thread on an unraveling spool of thoughts and emotions.

"We need to get him out of here fast," I said to Joseph, and he nodded in agreement, still in silent shock. He sniffled a little, quickly wiping away his tears to look strong and put together for anyone he passed.

He stood up and looked down at his robe, covered with blood as if he was the one beaten and tortured. There was going to be no hiding what he had done, unless he scrapped his robe. I didn't say a word, but his awestruck face spoke the word I was thinking. *Why?*

"Joseph, you're bleeding," I said, pointing at a fresh trail of blood flowing down his arm.

He didn't say anything but just shook his head. He glanced down at his arm and noticed the fresh wound. He watched as the blood trickled, as if amazed.

"Ready?" I asked him. He nodded and stooped down again. We wrapped our friend in a linen sheet to help with carrying and then we each stood up and carried our friend to his grave. The rocky hill of Golgotha tripped me a few times since it was dark and I couldn't see my footing, but we were both determined to not drop Jesus in front of his mother. "Where are we going?" I asked as Joseph finally looked up. He couldn't take his eyes off the clean white sheet quickly turning red.

"I'm going to put him in my tomb," he feebly said as we shifted for him to take the lead.

"My baby," Mary cried as we made it to the bottom of the hill and a few of her friends circled around her to keep her wobbly legs from losing all their balance.

I didn't know what was more painful, hearing my friend cry from the cross or seeing his mother cry now. A lump formed in my throat and stole the air from my chest. Taking in a deep breath, I did the best I could to regain some composure. I knew the walk to the tomb was going to be one that would drain me physically and emotionally.

I watched as Joseph periodically looked over his shoulder to make sure he wouldn't trip, but the majority of the time, he was watching the linen that encased our friend. I prayed as I walked. I prayed for the pain we were going through. I prayed for protection for the coming days. I prayed for God to protect us. But I mostly prayed so I could tune out Mary's heart-wrenching moans. I knew it was selfish for me to pray that, but I didn't know how I was going to make it. My body was already in shambles and I was crumbling a little more each time I heard her wail. A mother's cry is painful for anyone to listen.

We were nearing the tomb as someone ran up beside me and spit on the sheet. "Liar!" he screamed as we continued to walk at what felt like a snail's pace. I wanted to turn to the gentleman and ask him to stop, but I knew he wouldn't. There was going to be no silencing these people until we got Jesus in the tomb. And even then, there might still be people belittling him to Mary on a daily basis. The good thing about living in a small community was we had people to turn to. The bad thing about living in a small community was rumors and hurtful words spread faster than condolences.

I looked up at the sky and recalled the first time I approached Jesus. It had been under a darkened sky as well, but thankfully the moon had been shining during our first discussion. I had wanted to know more about this man that people were getting riled up about, so I went to him under the moonlight so no one else would ever find out. He spoke wisdom that baffled and confused, yet it also had a simplicity that befuddled and dumbfounded. Yet every time we parted company I felt like I had uncovered a new layer of who this Jesus was. When I thought I had finally figured him out, he would remove another layer. Lies have a tendency to topple over onto one another or implode inside themselves, but when he spoke, I never felt like he was speaking a lie. I always walked away with a feeling of renewal and restoration.

That was until today.

I felt destroyed in the middle of the ruins and was left staring at the bricks wondering, *What now? What do I think now?*

My flashback of memories disappeared as we entered Joseph's darkened tomb. One of the ladies entered with a torch in her hand and shone light into the bleakness, leaving nothing to our imagination.

Light usually brings warmth and protection, but this flame only solidified our broken hopelessness. We laid his body on a table in the center of the tomb, and Joseph bent down and picked up some jars in the corner. He unfolded the linen wrapped around Jesus' head. We didn't have long before we would have to leave. We didn't have enough time to properly bury him and would have to return in a couple of days.

I looked over at Mary who was trembling in Mary Magdalene's arms. I walked to the head of the table and trembled as I reached my hand out to remove the crown of thorns from his head. I gently raised his head, thinking the crown would fall off, but it was stuck into his scalp. The guards had smashed it hard into his tender scalp. Carefully, I tried to avoid the thorns, but no matter where I put my hand I felt the thistles scrape my skin. I finally had to succumb to the pain of grabbing a fistful of thorns to remove the cruel head piece. As I pulled I heard the eeriness of flesh parting from the body. When I lifted the crown up to the light to get rid of it, I saw pieces of flesh embedded into the thorns as it dripped blood.

"My baby," Mary moaned again as Joseph started to quickly pour the burial oils over Jesus' body.

Chapter 4

Mary – Mother of Jesus

"My baby," I cried looking down at my oldest child lying disfigured and battered from the wickedness the Roman guards inflicted. My eyes gushed more tears than I had ever cried before, and it seemed like my well of tears was never going to run dry.

Joseph started to sprinkle some incense and oils over my boy's body and the smells tickled my nostrils, conjuring up memories of when the guests from the East came into our home when he was just a little boy.

"We've come a long way following a star to give you these treasures," one of the kneeling men had said as they saw me and Jesus together. "Please, take our gifts of gold, frankincense, and myrrh."

I recalled the warm, woodsy fragrance of their gifts when they opened their jars as if it was yesterday. I had known my son was different. I had been approached by an angel, but this was the first time that someone else had confirmed his uniqueness.

I looked down and watched as Joseph started wiping away the dried blood around his face and the fragrance swirled within the tomb. The smell of the dampness quickly fled as the aromatic oils filled the tiny cave. But as I looked down, the words of the three guests came wafting into my head, words I had forgotten. "He who has been born King of the Jews. For we saw his star when it rose and have come to worship him."

"If he was the King of the Jews," I quietly muttered to myself, "then why did they kill him?"

"What, Mary?" Nicodemus asked, standing in the corner handing Joseph the jars of oil.

I didn't feel like repeating myself. I didn't want my words to be heard. I just wanted this whole thing to be a mistake and life to go back as normal. "No, no, no," I stammered as I realized this was not a mistake; this was not a dream I was going to wake from at any minute. This was reality. A sad, bitter, depressing reality.

Joseph tenderly wiped away the filth from Jesus' face. His face had aged years in just this one day. His welcoming gaze was a disjointed hodgepodge of wear and tear. I leaned over and brushed his hair. The cold wetness of his blood stuck to my hand, but I didn't care.

I looked around the tomb and was taken back to the moment when I met him for the first time in that lonely, smelly stable. I was terrified of being an expecting young mother and I knew my time was nearing. And then it happened. In the most unlikely of places, my first born came into the world. I remembered my husband, Joseph, God rest his soul, encouraging me. We were new to all this, but I would never forget those first few moments when we huddled together to look at our child. After we cleaned him up, I looked into his sleepy eyes and sang a lullaby that my mother used to sing to me. I brushed his brown curly locks and hummed the melody. I knew I was going to love him forever. But I guess that is how all mothers feel when they meet their child for the first time.

I traced my fingers down his face, cupping his cheeks like I had done many times when he was a young boy. "Now Jesus, you be a good, good boy," I would tell him, and he would always smile and nod his head.

He would look into my eyes lovingly and say, "Yes, Momma, I'll be a good boy."

Now I trailed my hands down his cheeks again, only this time I felt the stubble of his facial hair. I almost wanted to smile and laugh because even though he was thirty-three, he was still my little boy. Even though he was a fully grown man, he would always be my little Jesus. Ask any mother, and no matter the age of their child, they will always be their baby.

Joseph opened the linen cloth a little more, pouring some oil on the wounds on his chest. My heart sank when I saw the gaping rips and tears. I reached into the cloth and pulled out his arm. I wanted to hold my son's hand just one more time. My soul churned with pain when I saw the hole in his wrist. "My baby," I cried falling to my knees, kissing his wounds. I only wished my kisses could have healed his wounds like they used to when he would fall and scrape his knees as a toddler learning to walk.

"Come on, Jesus, get back up. You can do it. I'm right here," I would say, grabbing onto his hands and lifting him up to his feet. He would wrap his little hands around my fingers and I would walk him between my legs. He would laugh. I would smile. And we would walk hand in hand until he got the nerve to let go and take a few more steps on his own.

"I'm right here, baby," I whispered. "I'm still right here, holding your hand. Please get back up," I gushed. "Please, baby, please, please, Jesus, just stand back up. I know you can do it. I know you can." But through my tear-soaked eyelashes, I saw he didn't stand back up. He didn't grip my hand. He didn't laugh his contagious laugh. He continued to lie curled up in his sheet like he was going to go to sleep.

I swayed back and forth, as if rocking my little boy to sleep one final time. I started singing the lullaby I sung to him on our first night together in Bethlehem. I heard my friend Joseph say he was finished and we all needed to leave, but I wasn't ready.

"We need to leave, Mary," he said tenderly, but I wasn't ready to hear those words.

"Just give me a few more minutes," I said. I folded his arm back into the linen and started to swaddle him like I had thirty years ago. I continued to softly sing wrapping the white linen tightly around his wounded body. Leaning down I kissed his cheek. "Momma loves you," I said and then inched my lips toward his forehead, kissing him once again. "I will always love you."

I brushed his hair out of his eyes and stared at my sleeping child. I stood up and covered the sheet up to his neck, tightly binding him for a cold night's sleep. I looked down at his face and my vision was blurry. I couldn't see through the tears anymore.

"I can't do it!" I crumbled as I felt someone catch me from behind.

"He was a good man," she said as she raised the linen over Jesus' face. "A very good man."

Chapter 5

Mary Magdalene

"He was a good man," I said, using every ounce of my strength to lift the heavy sheet to cover my friend and savior. "A very good man." I looked at the sheet and wanted to rip it off of his body. I wanted him to show everyone that he was just tired and napping after an exhausting day.

I looked around the tomb, and the downcast faces sent a chill down my spine that froze me solid. I couldn't move. I couldn't speak. All I could do was recall the moment when I first met him.

I didn't recall the first words he'd said to me, but I would never forget the first words I remembered: "You're free, Mary."

I remembered looking around from the ground and seeing the amazed faces on my family members whose cheeks were wet from tears. I didn't recognize the voice, but he repeated it again. "You're free, Mary." This time my head turned up to his direction where I found a man stooping down, holding out an outstretched hand for me to grab.

Raising my body, I reached for his hand and noticed my arms and hands caked with dirt and mud. I didn't recall why I was so dirty, but something in his eyes told me to not worry about the dirt. As he helped me up from the filthy ground, I heard my family roar in excitement. I felt hugs and kisses in all directions from everyone. Someone brought my mother a jar of water, but instead of just washing my hands and arms, she tenderly took a rag and washed down my face and hair as the rest of my friends and family continued to surround me with love.

Yet, I hadn't understood why.

That was the really interesting thing about it. I had no recollection of why I was on the ground, covered in dirt. I didn't have any recent memories and I couldn't even recall what day it was.

After my mother had washed away the grime I noticed scratch marks on my arms. When my mother saw the shock on my face, she lovingly grabbed my arms and kissed them as if to remove the damage. I stood confused. I felt a warmth I hadn't felt in some time, but in the warmth there was also an uncertainty.

Why were people celebrating me? And who was this man that just helped me up? Did he rescue me from an attack? And if so, who attacked me? My head was running circles around itself.

The stranger walked up and the people around me hushed and stepped away from me. He stepped closer and took the rag from my mother. He dipped the rag into the cloudy water and gently washed it over my arms. "It's very nice to meet you, Mary. My name is Jesus," he said compassionately. "You were bound by evil forces beyond your control for some time doing self-harm. Those wounds you see were by your own hands. That is why your friends and family are rejoicing in your healing. You have not been yourself for some time. But now," he said with great authority, "now you are free and healed indeed."

My memory ended and I found myself back in the tomb, still frozen to the ground. I raised my arm to touch the hand that set me free. I couldn't see the wounds of my self-infliction. He set me free from the evil spirits that were possessing me and he healed my wounds so my arms were flawless.

My eyes started to water as I recalled that in one instant I was damaged and hurt, but in the next it was as if he wiped the wounds away from my hands and arms. I knew from that instant this man wasn't a normal man. He was the messiah. He had healed me when no one else could.

And yet, now here I was standing beside his dead body.

"I don't understand," I said feebly. "But he saved me." I didn't want to say the words audibly, but I had been thinking them for the last hour. I thought as he hung on the cross that at any minute he was going to get down and heal himself. I watched and waited for that moment. I knew beyond a reasonable doubt that if this man could help an ordinary woman like myself, then nothing was too hard for him.

Nothing.

"I don't understand either," a soft teenaged voice said behind me.

With those words, I finally broke down. I turned into his arms and felt his weak embrace. I crumbled under the avalanche of broken promises. It was as if a dam broke and I felt a tidal wave of pressure slam onto my back. I had stayed strong thinking Jesus was going to reveal his true self. I waited for the moment when he would rise from the dead like he had called forth the dead before him. But as this young man agreed with me, I felt a coldness I hadn't felt in a very long time.

Doubt became my master.

Chapter 6
John

"I don't understand either," I said as my insides broke into a million little pieces. I don't know who embraced whom, but if Mary of Magdala wasn't within an arm's reach from me, I was about to topple over. It was as if we both collided into one another's arms, and each of our opposing weights held the other up.

"I just don't understand," I muttered to myself as my eyes swelled with tears. I was trying to be strong for the women, but this was a weight that almost seemed impossible. He was my friend, but he was more than a friend. I loved him like a brother. Even before he called me to follow him as I was fishing that day three years earlier, I knew there was something different about him. Even my mother saw there was something special about Jesus.

Looking down at my friend, I recalled many incidents in the last few years I couldn't explain, but one memory sprung forward with overwhelming confusion. I remembered it so vividly, when Jesus took me, Peter, and my brother James up a mountain. There was no way a simple magic man could shine such a brilliant light and make his clothes transform instantly before our eyes. Yet, Jesus shone brighter than the sun. It was as if the light was coming from him. It was as if he was the light.

I had stared, mesmerized. The sight was intoxicating. I couldn't look away. It was as if the light was drawing me into a different place and time. Then two other men appeared. Jesus called them Moses and Elijah and they spoke like great men of faith. I looked over at Peter and my brother and they, too, were awestruck. Only Peter could get a word out, but right when he spoke, it was like a voice from the Heavens silenced the world. I would never forget that voice or the words.

"This is my beloved Son, with whom I am well-pleased; listen to him."

I didn't know what came over me, but I knew, beyond every logical thought, that God had just spoken. The actual voice of God was speaking about my friend Jesus. We all fell down immediately. I fell for fear. I wasn't totally sure why Peter and James were on the ground, but all I knew was that when I looked up, they were kneeling on the ground beside me. I never spoke to James about the incident, since Jesus asked us not to speak about it to anyone when we were coming down the mountain. I'd often wondered what he thought. I couldn't see my older brother being scared, because big brothers were never scared of anything. Yet, it left me feeling both scared and confused. Then as quickly as it happened, it passed away like nothing. Moses and Elijah were gone. Jesus was back in his normal, tattered robe without a glorious light. And I was left with a feeling that Jesus was just as the voice had said: "My beloved Son."

And now he was dead. I shook my head and quickly wiped my eyes before a tear started to fall. Mary and I parted from our embrace as we all stood and waited for the first person to make a move.

"We need to go," Joseph once again said and we all nodded in agreement that it was time.

I went over to Mary, wrapped my arms around her, lifted her up, and allowed her to lean on me just as I had held onto her during the last couple of hours. She looked up at me with a loving gaze, and I stared back at her with compassion and a renewal of strength as I remembered the last words Jesus had said to me.

"Behold, your mother!" Jesus had said from the cross. His last words were filled with love for his mother. Even as he was dying on the cross he was still thinking of others.

As we looked into each other's eyes it was as if I heard what Jesus said to Mary, "Woman, behold, your son!" My knees slightly buckled, but I quickly regained the strength. I thought Jesus had been only thinking of his love and protection for his mother, but he was also thinking of his love and companionship for me. Maybe he knew that with him gone, my best friend was gone, and I needed a piece of him as a reminder of his love. What better tangible reminder than his mother?

I leaned down and whispered softly into her ear, "I love you, Mother."

I then looked to the woman on the other side of Mary, and mouthed the same words. "I love you, Mother."

My mother's lips quivered as she replied, "I love you too, John."

Chapter 7

Salome – Wife of Zebedee and Mother of James and John

"I love you too, John," I mouthed, as I didn't want to speak audibly for everyone to hear.

I moved my attention from John to Mary, who was clutching my hand. We started walking to the tomb's opening, but the outside looked as dark as in the tomb. I looked back one last time and my heart was torn. There under the sheet was my friend's son, my son's friend, and a man whom I believed was going to do what he said he would. My heart was hurt looking at Mary. I felt so sorry for what she was going through. A mother should never have to witness her child dying, especially by that method.

It may have been selfish, but I was glad it was Jesus who died and not my own son. As I thought it, I knew it was wrong to be thinking that way. On one side of the coin I was grieving with my friend for her loss, but on the other side I was celebrating that I had more time with my own sons.

We slowly stepped out of the tomb, and I still held onto Mary, letting her feel my touch of compassion. I wondered if she knew how lucky I felt. Would she be feeling the way I was if our roles were reversed? Probably not, because Mary was always a better person than I was. She was nurturing and kind from an early age. She was something to be admired, even when we were children. I never told her that, but she had an unexplainable air about her. I had always wanted to be like her.

That was until now. Now, I was fortunate to not be her.

I glanced over at John, who continued to look straight ahead at the path he had walked down thousands of times in his life. I wondered what he was thinking. Isn't that what good mothers did? They looked out for their children and fixated on their well-being.

I couldn't stop myself, so I looked back at the lonely tomb. I could barely see the white linen sheet covering Jesus' feet. A thought pranced into my head of a time when I had spoken to Jesus, once again, about the well-being of my sons.

"What do you want?" Jesus had asked me as I knelt before him.

"Say that these two sons of mine are to sit, one at your right hand and one at your left, in your kingdom," I had pleaded. I only wanted the best for my sons. What mother wouldn't have done the same if they were in my situation? I knew they were courageous. I knew they were loyal. I had taught them well as young boys and they had grown into mature, knowledgeable young men. Men I would gladly follow if they were fellow leaders of Jesus' kingdom.

But Jesus never nodded yes. He just asked a strange question.

"You do not know what you are asking. Are you able to drink the cup that I am to drink?" he asked.

I wanted to ask what cup he spoke of, but my sons wouldn't let me voice my question. They quickly answered.

"We are able," James and John had said, almost in unison as they looked at one another and agreed.

"You will drink my cup, but to sit at my right hand and at my left is not mine to grant, but it is for those for whom it has been prepared by my Father," Jesus answered.

I was so pleased with my sons. I knew they were capable of anything handed to them. I was only trying to help my sons move up. Sometimes people have to push their way to the top to be noticed. Once they are noticed then they can prove themselves. It's hard proving worth when no one is watching. I know what I did caused some division among the men as they quickly started questioning and harassing James and John.

"What makes them special?" someone had asked, and the others all agreed.

"If my mother was here and asked the question, would you have replied the same way?" someone else had asked as I was shot a degrading look.

Jesus quickly went into teaching to calm the commotion. His teachings always pierced my heart when he spoke.

Now that he was dead, I realized it was useless to have asked him about giving my sons seats in his kingdom. It was stupid of me to start thinking of titles to give my sons as they ruled beside Jesus. I was foolish to have believed that a change for the better was coming.

I squeezed Mary's hand to remind myself of the blessing I still had. I may have lost one dream, but at least I could start to dream again of something else for my sons. Sadly, Mary couldn't say that now.

Her dream was over.

"Can someone help me?" Joseph asked as he stood beside a stone large enough to seal the entrance of the tomb. "I can't do it alone."

Nicodemus and John quickly ran to help Joseph and used all of their remaining strength. The large stone barely started to roll. They

29

heaved with all their might until finally the closure was complete. There were no gaping holes so no animals or pests could get through before they could finalize the burial preparations.

"No," said a light voice somewhere in the garden.

I turned my head to see if I could see anyone, but it was too dark. It must have been the wind. Who else would be out at a time like this?

Chapter 8
Peter

"No," I softly moaned from a distance as I hid behind a bush and saw three men close the tomb. I clasped my hand over my mouth, quickly falling onto the ground and silently weeping into the dirt to stifle my cries. My trickling tears started to form a small patch of mud where my head pressed into the ground.

God, why? I internally screamed. I wanted an answer. How could God allow an innocent man to die? How could God sit idly by and let Jesus be killed for a crime he didn't commit? With each tear that fell down my nose, another question arose. I raised my head to watch a small group of my friends huddle around Mary as if protecting her from the unrelenting wind and rain pelting my back.

I wanted to be in that group. I so dearly wanted to be a part of their grieving circle, but I couldn't pick myself up off the ground. The agony and regret of fleeing the scene and denouncing my friend, not once, but three times was too much for me move on.

I had watched the crowds begin to gather earlier today, lining the road that all criminals walked to their impending death on the place of the skull. I couldn't get up close enough to watch Jesus shuffle his tired feet as he carried the massive wooden beams. I had slinked off to a hidden narrow alleyway and sat with my knees to my chest, heaving a few painful breaths. I didn't betray him like someone else had, but I denied him.

"I'm so sorry, Jesus," I whispered for the first time as I stared at the enclosed tomb. I was still too scared to leave the safety of the camouflaged bush. I had tried to say those words earlier today, but I couldn't. I just couldn't. All I could do was stare into the eyes of my Lord.

Even though I hadn't stood up with the crowd to watch Jesus stumble down the agonizing walk, it was like destiny wanted me to witness his suffering. I heard him moan in exhaustion as I watched his feet get purposely tripped by one of the mockers that wanted him to fall.

And he fell hard. I saw his bleeding scalp from where those sharp thorns had dug into his skin. I didn't move. I held my breath thinking he wouldn't know I was there in the alley. He wouldn't turn his head in my direction to look me in the face behind the forest of legs that separated us. He wouldn't find me safely hiding in the shadows as he laid in the sun-drenched rocky road.

But he had.

He'd turned his head directly at me as if he knew I was watching him. I didn't want him to see me, but I knew he did. Our eyes locked for what felt like an eternity. He looked at me unfazed.

That look of disengagement caused my heart to stop. I wished he had looked at me with sorrow or disgust. I wanted him to scream my name, to curse my existence for turning my back on him like he warned me I would. I wanted him to spit into the ground as if spitting into my selfish face. But he didn't. He looked at me without any life in his eyes.

That look wrecked me. It was like he had given up on himself and on me. That look of detachment was one I would see every time I closed my eyes.

Now, in front of his tomb, I watched the group turn down the path to head home. I stumbled to my shaky legs, but my balance was off kilter and I felt like the world was spinning. I wondered if I would even be able to walk, but I had to.

I had to touch the stone that separated me from my beloved friend. I escaped the security of the bushes and cautiously walked forward. I couldn't see anyone. The only sounds were the occasional booming thunder and the pelting of raindrops on my shoulder.

I took a few steps but fell forward. My legs couldn't do it, yet I had to feel the stone. I had to get there. I looked up and started to crawl like a toddler. My knees were scraping against the rocks scattered in the path. My hands were getting covered in another layer of wet dirt with each forward motion. I looked up and saw the large stone was an outstretched arm's length away. I leaned forward and raised my trembling hand. I closed my eyes and strained to feel the hardness.

My heart slowed as I felt the cold rock that kept the death of my friend at bay. I pressed my weight onto it and used it to raise myself up, almost hugging the piece of granite like a long-lost friend.

"Jesus," I moaned, embracing the hard exterior. I heard a stick break on the ground behind me. I froze against the rock, knowing I was caught.

"Who are you?" a man asked.

But I didn't answer. I didn't turn around. I fled the scene.

Once again.

Chapter 9
Longinus

I walked down the quiet road from Golgotha to the burial ground of Jesus, as questions filled my head. I found a man leaning against the stone at the entrance of the grave. "Who are you?" I asked. He didn't answer but quickly darted out of eyesight. I raised my torch to try to find him, but it was useless with the flame made fragile by the wind and rain.

I stepped closer to the tomb and examined the surroundings. I was stalling because I still didn't understand why I came to the gravesite of this man I didn't know. I didn't know what led me to seek out his resting place, but I knew I had to follow my gut. My instincts had never let me down before. There were many times during battles when I knew someone was swinging their sword behind my back, or a flying arrow was just a few inches to my left or right, or I was about to be double-teamed in hand-to-hand combat. My gut had never let me down before and I knew I had to follow on that uncertainty.

I traced my hands along the stone that blocked the entrance and felt the heaviness and hardness of the sealant. I also felt a heaviness and hardness of my heart after years of staying professional with the criminals I encountered. This was the first time I had ever journeyed to the grave of someone I helped execute. As I stood in front of the stone, I wondered why I was there. Not as a philosophical question of existence, but one of physical location.

"Why did I come to the grave of a man I never knew before?"

There were many people that had parted ways to the next realm of existence, whatever that may be, but I seldom went to the gravesite for friends and family members. So, why was I there now for a mere stranger?

I couldn't answer the question cycling through my brain like a spinning wheel. I couldn't come up with a definitive answer that seemed logical and cohesive.

Standing against the rock, I turned around to see the outlay of the land. There was a small garden near the tomb cut in half by the narrow strip of dirt that formed a path towards the city. I tried to look into the distance, but it was useless to see anything beyond the garden due to the midnight stormy sky. Occasionally, a flash of lightning would streak overhead, shining a glimmer of light to see the horizon, but it wasn't enough for my mind to remember in detail what I had just witnessed.

I started to contemplate the question nagging at my heart: Who was this man and what made him believe he was the King of the Jews? Was that a title he gave himself? Because apparently the Jews watching his death didn't agree with the sign hanging above his head. They mocked him belligerently, not as a leader, but as a fool.

Was this Jesus a fool?

He died with a handful of people, some of whom I assume were his followers, but could having a following of ten people be enough to issue a decree as a king? I shook my head. I didn't have a full picture of who this Jesus was. I had watched as Pilate questioned him, and his answers had seemed logical. He didn't seem like a lunatic. He wasn't wickedly charismatic trying to sway the judgment from death to life. He didn't even beg for his life like every other criminal before him.

It was as if he knew his fate. And a horrible fate it was.

And then when he was dying on the cross, he actually asked his father to forgive the crowd for what they were doing. I didn't recall seeing his father, but he could have been one of the two men that carried him down the hill. If that wasn't crazy enough, he was also comforting one of the other criminals dying on another cross. Who would do such a thing when each breath was precious? I heard him say, "Truly I say to you, today you will be with me in paradise."

I didn't understand why he was lying to the man. Where was this paradise he mentioned, because neither one of them got off the cross to go there.

Each of them died.

I could have easily written him off as a liar or a lunatic, but something in my gut nixed those conclusions. This man behind the stone died an innocent man. I didn't know why I believed that, but once again, it was something my gut was telling me.

And now my instinct was telling me I needed to leave this plot of land as soon as possible. I waved my torch in front of my eyes to see some of the path ahead of me. I started walking as a flash of lightning illuminated the sky. In the distance I saw the hill where Jesus had been executed. I squinted my eyes and saw there was still one body hanging on a cross on the left side of the hill. His family had never come to get him. Sad to die alone.

I left the path of solitude and entered the outskirts of Jerusalem where I could see people's silhouettes from the candles lit in the homes. Walking through the rain, I started to feel cold from the chill of the wind and my drenched coverings. I leaned against a home, hoping to find a small piece of shelter from the storm since my home was still further into the city.

"So it really happened?" I heard a woman's voice ask sympathetically behind the window pane. "He's dead?"

Chapter 10

Rebekka – Wife of Jude, the Brother of Jesus

I looked into Jude's eyes as he sat nonchalantly at the table, getting ready to partake in his supper. "So it really happened?" I asked solemnly, wiping my hands after the preparations. "He's dead?"

He didn't have to answer. I already knew.

Silently, he lifted his eyes and watched as my composure crumbled like statues made of dirt and water. I felt like the world around my feet was eroding like the creations I used to make as a little girl.

"What did you expect?" he asked with a degrading look. He had always been annoyed at my loyalty to Jesus. Always.

"How can you act like that?" I asked agitatedly.

"Like what?" he said still sitting at the table, looking at me with judgmental eyes. "Like the brother of a man who finally got what he deserved?"

"He was your brother!" I lashed out, stomping my feet and shaking my fists into the air. "He was your brother!"

Jude continued to sit, tapping his fingernails along the wooden table he and Jesus had made four years ago. The sturdy table was a fine piece of craftsmanship. I, on the other hand, was a lopsided woman on two flimsy legs.

"The way he's treated us the last three years, I'm amazed you can still support him," he said without raising his voice to me. "That you still believe he's something special."

"The way he treated us?" I asked in shock.

"Wake up, Rebekka," he said, finally standing up and walking in my direction. "He took off roaming around, God knows where, saying ridiculous things to find simple-minded gullible people to be his followers. He's been playing me all my life."

"Don't say that," I said with broken speech. My breath was lost inside my chest. "Don't say that."

"Why not?" he asked crossing his arms to stand his guard.

I couldn't look at him anymore. I turned around and gripped a ceramic jug. I wanted to pick up the heavy container filled with wine for special occasions when a memory came wafting as I leaned over and smelled the liquid grapes.

Three years ago, almost all of Jude's family and friends had gathered for a wedding in Cana. I loved weddings, especially being there and witnessing such a joyous occasion with the love of my life by my side. On the third or fourth day, the host of the wedding ran out of wine.

I was beside Mary when she said to Jesus, "They have no wine."

I was confused why she would even brought up the subject to Jesus. I didn't think Mary was the type to ridicule someone for their lack of preparedness, and the comment to Jesus was very strange to my ears.

Then Jesus said something even stranger. "Woman, what does this have to do with me? My hour has not come."

I remember standing awkwardly beside Mary. Jude was with the rest of the men of his family across the plaza. "Do whatever he tells you," Mary told the servants.

I was once again confused wondering what Jesus had to do with wine. But to my amazement, he followed his mother's orders.

Jesus walked away with the servants and found some large empty jars. I was intrigued and a little curious so I followed. "Fill the jars with water," he'd said as the servants obliged and filled up each of the jars to the very top. "Now draw some out and take it to the master of the feast."

I remember watching from a distance as the master took a sip of the water. His eyes showed amazement as he commanded the servants to freely pour the newly found wine. I quickly ran to one of the water jugs and dipped my empty cup. But water didn't fill my cup. It was succulent wine. The best that I had ever tasted.

I looked over at Jesus expecting him to give me a smile, or a wink, or a nod, but he just went back to enjoy the company of the wedding feast. He hadn't put on a show or announce to everyone what he had just accomplished.

But I'd seen it. I saw what he did.

"How?" I asked, back in my own kitchen, looking down into the half empty jug of wine in my hands.

"What do you mean how?" Jude asked bewildered. "You know how."

"No," I said turning around raising my hands with the jug in them. "How do you explain this?"

Jude looked at me quizzically. We stood just a few steps apart, but it felt like we were on different sides of the world.

"I don't know what you are talking about, Rebekka," he said taking one step closer, but still too far away to reach me.

"You never knew what I was I talking about," I said as I lost feeling in my hands. I tried to recover, but it was too little, too late. I watched as the jug collided with the ground and broke in three large pieces as splotches of wine escaped. "You never believed me."

"Honey," he said, running over to my side and bending down with me to pick up the broken pieces. "I believe you think you saw something. But Jesus," he stopped and held my hand, my trembling weak hand, "he was playing you."

"No," I said with tears filling my hopeful eyes. I trusted Jesus. I really did. I wanted him to be everything everyone was saying he was. But I also loved Jude. He was my husband. I was always in the middle, caught in the crossfire of Jude's snide remarks and Jesus' kind words. Jesus always proved himself true to me, but Jude never saw it. Jude was blind to the mystery of who Jesus was. And maybe, maybe I was just blinded by what I hoped the answer was.

"He played me too," he said remorsefully.

Chapter 11
Jude

"He played me too," I said looking into my loving wife's eyes. My heart broke seeing her in such a fragile state, yet I felt vindicated. All my life I had been the little brother of the best son who never did anything wrong. I was always the one who couldn't measure up to the perfect standards they believed Jesus set. I was always the one who, no matter how hard I tried, couldn't reach the elusive, impossible goal, because Jesus, too, never reached it. It was sad to say, but he played everyone.

He was the great manipulator.

"You need to go check on your mother," Rebekka said as we stood up, hand in hand. She knew I loved her. She knew I would do anything for her. I may not have always agreed with her theories and thoughts, but at the end of the day, I was on her side, faithfully.

"I will go now, before it gets too late," I said leaning my head down to kiss my wife. I hoped she knew I loved her more than my life itself. "When I come home, we can celebrate Passover if you want."

As the words left my mouth, I recalled a Passover almost twenty years earlier. I was very young, but I could still recall the vivid details. Jesus had just turned twelve and the entire family went to Jerusalem for the feast. In the celebrations we had, it was easy to get lost with all the friends and family, and Jesus got lost.

I remember Father and Mother searching for him frantically for a few days, but no one knew where Jesus was. Finally, we went back to the temple and found him listening to the teachers and asking them questions.

"Jesus!" My father had commanded. Jesus calmly turned around and gave his parents his undivided attention.

"Yes, Father," I remember Jesus answering innocently.

"Son, why have you treated us so? Behold, your father and I have been searching for you in great distress," my mother had said forcefully, yet with a mother's love.

I was ready for my parents to scold him. Even though I was very young, I had already learned Jesus was the perfect son and I was just there taking up space. But now, now I was going to enjoy the sight of their realization that Jesus was just like everyone else. There had been no reason to put him on a pedestal. I watched, waiting eagerly for Jesus to crumble, to beg for forgiveness, to say he was sorry. But he didn't.

"Why were you looking for me? Did you not know that I must be in my Father's house?" Jesus said and then turned to the teachers and bid them farewell. We all left together in silence.

I thought Father and Mother were going to punish Jesus for causing them three days of searching, but he didn't get in trouble. I watched in annoyance, knowing if I had wandered off for just an hour without telling them where I was going, I would have been reprimanded. But not Jesus.

As we returned home, Jesus obeyed every word Father and Mother said to him. He never back-talked. He never raised his voice. He just listened and did as the perfect Jesus always did.

I had looked over at my slightly older brother, James, who was also annoyed by the whole charade. As we journeyed home, I even looked over at my mother and she had an expression on her face that astonished me. She didn't look angry or upset. Her eyes didn't radiate any scorn or resentment. It was a look of pure joy and happiness. It was the look she had on her face any time Jesus was around.

I hardly ever got that look.

Shaking off the memory, I stepped outside of my home and walked a few houses over. I tried to get past the feeling of never being good enough. What made it worse was Jesus was always there to console me. He never made me feel like I was less than him. He was always the one to defend me when I messed up. He was always the one who encouraged me to be better than what everyone thought I could be.

I hated him for that more than anything else. I would had rather him be rude, insensitive, and presumptuous. A living, breathing tyrant who made me learn to always watch my back. I knew he was always watching my back, maybe not in the way big brothers were supposed to watch their younger brother. But I knew. I knew he had a reason for the way he acted. And he did it very well.

I lightly tapped on the door before entering. "Mother," I said as John greeted me with a hug.

"Where have you been?" he asked brushing off the rain from my head. "Your mother needed you."

Chapter 12
John

"Where have you been?" I asked Jude, astonished by his lack of respect for his grieving mother. "Your mother needed you."

"I'm here now," Jude snidely remarked, more interested in warming himself by the fire than consoling his wounded mother.

"Jude, my boy," Mary moaned from the sitting area, surrounded by Mary Magdalene, Salome, and a few other family members, friends, and neighbors. She reached her arms up, begging her son to give her his undivided attention and love.

I watched as he went down to one of his knees and hugged his mother compassionately, but he didn't look saddened or grief-stricken. He just looked flat, as if being with his mother was a duty at this moment in time and he was only there out of obligation.

"I just can't believe it," Mary gushed her tears on top of his head as she caressed his dark curly hair. "He looked so..." She stopped and inhaled a deep breath and tried to finish. "So..." she tried again, but she couldn't find the right word.

"I'm sorry for what he's put you through, Mother," Jude said. As I heard those words, it was like a slap in the face to everyone in the room.

"Put her through?" I said in shock with a feeling of outrage coursing through my being.

"Yes," Jude nodded as he looked up at me with cold, distant eyes. "He's put her through more heartache than anyone." He turned his attention away from me and cupped his mother's face.

My breathing increased as my nose started to flare with fiery anger. "How can you say that about your own brother who's only been dead a couple of hours?"

Jude stood up and walked over to me until our noses were just a few inches apart. "Until you have known him as long as I have, I don't care what you think. And since he's dead," he said shrugging his shoulders, "I guess I will never care what you think."

"Jude!" Mary screeched as my tongue was tied by his lack of decency.

"It's true, Mother!" Jude exploded. It was as if he'd had thirty years of anger to let free. "You have always treated Jesus differently, thinking he was better than the rest of us, but Jesus wasn't. He just connived you into thinking he was something special."

"Jude, stop that," Mary Magdalene softly hushed as she embraced Mary, covering her ears to block the hurtful words coming out of her son's lips. "Just stop."

"Why?" Jude ranted even more. "Wake up, Mary! He's dead and the world didn't stop. It's going to keep on going like he was nothing special. Because he wasn't."

I watched in horror at the disrespect being slung around the tiny room. "If you don't stop," I started as Jude walked over to me.

"What, John?" Jude said cynically. "What in the world are you going to do? Hide behind your mother like you've been doing all your life?"

"That's enough!" I shouted. My grieving had ended and retaliation was bubbling to the surface. "Just leave before you say something you may regret."

"Oh, John," he smiled wickedly. "I'm not the one who has any regrets, unlike you."

"And what do you mean by that?" I snapped, ignoring the women's pleas to end the discussion.

He ignored their heartfelt notions to cease the debate as well. "Well, I never thought Jesus was going to accomplish much in his life. Unlike you, I haven't spent the last three years wasting my life following his lies and manipulations. I've been living my life with wide eyes seeing through the sheep's clothing he has worn. I've lived my life without putting any false hope in a so-called traveling prophet who was going to redeem me. He used you for his own personal agenda. You have no idea how much joy he got out of exploiting you and your naivety. That's the Jesus I grew up with. His life was a big hoax. And you're just another pawn in his elaborate scheme for fame and recognition."

"Stop it!" I shouted. "Just stop it!"

"John, wake up!" he screamed back in my face. "Jesus is dead, and in a few days no one is going to care that he's gone."

"I'll care."

Chapter 13

Mary

"I'll care," I said looking up into the eyes of my living, breathing son. "I will always care," I said softly as my eyes continued to fill with tears. "Please, Jude, please don't say that about your brother. Please don't say that."

I saw the look in Jude's eyes that told me he didn't feel the same way I did.

"Mom, I'm sorry, but he was a liar," Jude said unremorsefully. His anger had left and now he was left standing in the middle of a room of people who opposed him. People who disagreed with his biases. Yet, everyone in the room still loved him.

"I love you, Jude, but please stop," I said with a broken spirit and quivering speech.

Mary Magdalene continued to hold my numb, weak hand, as she tenderly squeezed it to let me know she was there. I turned my eyes away from my son's that looked sickened and befuddled at my continual support of Jesus. I needed to find some solace in this tragedy. I needed to find compassion and not a raising voice or pointing finger. I found the depth of sympathy in the hazel colored eyes of Mary Magdalene.

In the last few years she had turned into a loyal friend and confidant. Even though she was my daughter's age, she had something special that radiated from her, causing everyone to draw toward her with intrigue. I needed that strong pull into her arms of love and mercy.

"You've always sided with him," Jude muttered under his breath as he walked away from where we were sitting and sulked in a nearby bedroom.

Those words hurt. I knew Jude believed what he said, but I never loved any one of my children more than another. Yes, Jesus was an easier son to raise. He was respectful, obedient, never a troublemaker, and very conscientious. I wish I could have said my other sons were model citizens, but that would have been a lie.

But just because they didn't mirror Jesus, didn't mean I loved them any less. They were all my children. Any mother could say one child was the smartest, or the funniest, or the hardest working, but to say one was more loved than another? I simply wasn't capable of that. I loved all my children evenly. Even if they didn't believe it.

"He's just hurt," Mary Magdalene whispered kindly into my ear as she rested her head on my shoulder.

I listened to her words, hoping they were true, but I knew Jude's words were ones he'd been waiting to say for years. It wasn't because of some suddenly tarnished emotions.

"No," I said shaking my head. "He means it."

I looked around the room. I was in the middle of a circle of loved ones that cared so much for me. Yet, I felt a rift growing wider. I had always dismissed Jude's and James' slanderous words about Jesus. I had tried to overlook them. I even occasionally denounced their claims of preferential treatment, but with every word I would say, I could see a brick being built on a wall that separated us.

It was a great chasm that silently broke my heart when I would see my other children snicker at Jesus behind his back. Yet, Jesus never retaliated at their remarks or schemed revenge. In an act of selfless love for his family Jesus continued to take the high road. Yet his siblings only continued to harbor more hate, gradually boiling since childhood. A sickening question flashed through my mind. I didn't want to know the answer, but I had to ask it.

"Get Jude," I said to John who was standing along the wall.

"Now?" he asked, puzzled and a little apprehensive.

I nodded my head as John left to the adjoining room. The two men returned with Jude slinking in with drooping shoulders and a heightened sense of concern.

"Where were you today?" I asked, hoping that Jude wouldn't answer the way I expected.

"Why do you want to know?" he asked, dodging the question.

"Just tell me, Jude. Where were you today?"

He looked around the room as if looking for a place to escape. His sunken shoulders quickly straightened as he looked at John standing beside him.

"You don't want to know, Mother," he answered in a heated breath. "Don't ask unless you really want to know."

My body tensed. His words were covered in hostility. His body was engulfed in the awareness that everyone else in the room knew where he was earlier today.

"Tell me you didn't, Jude," I pleaded, but my words fell on deaf ears.

An uncaring expression slithered down his face. "What does it matter anyways?" he asked unsympathetically. "Your precious son didn't see me in the crowd."

50

My chin fell to my chest as my heart broke a little more. I couldn't hold back the tears. It was one thing to silently wish for revenge on your relative, but it was another to cheer for your own brother to be crucified.

"I'm leaving," Jude said coldly as he stomped towards the door.

"Jude, tell me you didn't!"

Chapter 14

John

"Jude, tell me you didn't!" I yelled following him out the front door. "Jude! Stop!" He continued to walk ahead of me, ignoring my shouts. "Jude! How could you?"

He stopped and turned around, looking me squarely in the eyes without any hesitation. "How could I what? Do what was right?"

I stood flabbergasted. I looked around and noticed the darkened street still being pelted by rain under the blackened sky. The only light came through cracks in doors and windows from neighboring homes. My breath was stolen at the audacity of his words. My heart was swelling in rage at the authoritative tone with which he said the cruel words.

"How can you say what you did was right? He was your kin!" I said hatefully, barking back with venom-filled words. "He was your brother!"

"He was no brother to me!" he shouted, stepping closer until I could smell the hate on his breath.

"He was to me!" I exclaimed, spraying his face with my emotion-fueled words.

He shook his head, clenching his jaw, but he didn't care about sheltering his words. He was letting them fly. "Look around, John! Just open your eyes and look around!" He circled me like a lion watching an injured antelope. "Where are the rest of your so-called brothers?"

I flinched. He saw my shadowed face and grinned wickedly.

"Yeah, John, wake up! They realized Jesus was just using them too. You're just the last one to figure it out!"

I couldn't speak. I didn't know what to say as breath began to fill my empty lungs.

"Come on, man! I know you see it! No one else came to watch him die," he said slowly, as if letting the poisonous words seep into every part of my brain, "except for you." He stopped pacing around me until we were once again face to face. "And why do you think that is?"

I didn't want to answer that question. I didn't want to consider it. I wanted to give them excuses for fleeing or deserting me at the execution. But no matter what excuse I came up with, it was never enough to ease my troubled mind.

"Just stop," I softly said, trying to tune out his bullying tactics.

"Stop what, John?" he asked menacingly. "Saying you're all alone now? That your band of brothers won't even look you in the eyes if they saw you on the street tomorrow? That the life you were imagining with Jesus as a ruler is now over? That you've wasted the last three years of your life following a man who never had a plan, except to lure simple-minded people into believing he was the Messiah?"

"Just stop!" I pleaded again, as I stood teetering on a cliff of rage. He was rocking me back and forth, and I didn't know how long I could keep it inside.

"Get on with your life, John!" he said as if talking to a little kid wasting his life daydreaming. "He was nothing special. Just like you. Maybe that's why you two stuck so close together. You were easy to sway to his thinking because you were never a man thinking on your own. You always followed your mother's orders, and then when Jesus came, you followed his. You're just another sad, sad follower who was willing to follow a man to your own demise."

I looked at him and clenched my fists. They were shaking with untapped rage and fury.

He glanced down and saw my trembling hands. "I don't even think you have the guts to do anything with those, so just put them away *little boy.*"

When he called me *little boy*, I was ready to show him what I was made of. I lifted my fists. Aimed. And punched with all my might.

I punched with the rage of him calling me *little boy*.

I punched with the hurt of my friends not supporting Jesus as he suffered and died.

I punched with the animosity of the Jewish council executing my friend.

But mostly, I punched with my fear that Jude might be right.

Maybe I was just a follower who never thought for himself.

Jude tried to block the punches I was throwing, but I didn't stop. I felt my fist colliding with his flesh. I heard him groan with each punch. I felt a little trickle of blood oozing from a few new cuts, but I didn't stop. I didn't want to stop.

Jude may have thought I was a boy a minute ago, but I was showing him I was a man now. I may have only been a teenager, but I was also a fully grown man.

As I continued my rampage, he was only able to get two good shots in before he fell to the ground. But I didn't stop. My legs started kicking into his side.

54

"How's it feel, Jude?" I asked with shallow breath. "How does it feel now?"

He didn't answer but rolled his body into a ball, covering his head with his arms.

"Who's the boy now?" I screamed. "Who's the little boy now?"

"John," a familiar voice said behind me. "Stop!"

Chapter 15

Peter

"John," I said running up seeing my friend attacking a man on the street. "Stop!"

"But," John panted as he continued to kick the man on the ground, "he said... he said..."

I grabbed John and shoved him away from the stranger lying in the dirt. Leaning down, I checked on the man as he uncurled his arms from his head. "Jude?"

I reached down and helped him to his feet.

"You okay?" I asked Jude as he silently nodded. He started to brush himself off when I caught a blur of John moving toward us. I stepped into the middle of the two men and deflected the punch John threw at Jude.

"Who's the boy now?" John hissed in Jude's direction before turning away and walking down the darkened street toward Mary's home.

"What happened?" I asked Jude who started walking the other direction down the quiet road.

"He lost it," Jude said, shrugging his shoulders nonchalantly.

"Did he hurt you?"

"Hurt?" he laughed comically as he adjusted his jaw where John had gotten a few good jabs in. "Surprised me, yes, but not hurt."

I turned around and saw that John had disappeared into the blackness of the darkened road. All I could hear was the continuing rain splashing the puddles that were scattered on the ground. "Need any help home?" I asked Jude, but he brushed off my offer.

"Just leave, Peter," he said cruelly and walked away.

I stood still watching Jude hobble down the road, but something in my gut said I needed to walk the other way. I made it past a few homes before John stepped out of the shadows where he'd been hiding.

"Why weren't you there today?" John asked solemnly as I jumped back startled.

I didn't want to answer. I felt all my regret coming back. I had been in hiding for the last twenty-four hours and now I was face to face with my choices.

"Why weren't you there today?" he asked again, this time more forcefully as he came closer to me.

I shook my head with my eyes closed. I didn't feel like seeing the judgmental look of disgust on his face.

"Say something!" he angrily hissed as he pushed me back into the wall.

I felt the hardness against my back as the palm of his hand pressed into my chest.

"What do you want me to say?" I asked hastily. "It's not like it will change anything."

"Just tell me," he said bluntly. "Why weren't you there with us today?"

I shook my head and looked down at the pooled water at my feet. I didn't see it coming, but I felt it.

John threw another punch, hitting my left cheek with such force that the back of my skull slammed into the wall behind me. That was when everything went black.

I remembered sliding to the ground and faintly hearing footsteps leaving. I tried to open my eyes, but my vision was blurred, and I couldn't make out anything. I lifted my head from the puddle of water and waited for the splitting headache to pass. The coolness of the water actually helped alleviate some of the sudden pain.

I heard a couple of men's voices coming up the road. Then, between the rumbling thunder, I could hear two sets of footsteps. I looked over and saw two torches heading my direction, breaking through the fog and darkness. Their accent wasn't from this area. As they neared, I could make out a Roman soldier's uniform. I wasn't ready to be seen, so I moved my legs and scurried behind a barrel. I could clearly hear the two soldiers talking and my heart started to beat faster. I had been filled with so much regret today I didn't let any other emotion surface. Until now. Now, I felt rage as I overheard part of their conversation.

"Have you ever felt anything for one of the men you've executed? Because that man, Jesus... I have a strange feeling about what I've done."

Chapter 16

Longinus

"Have you ever felt anything for one of the men you've executed? Because that man, Jesus…" I paused and thought for a moment. "I have a strange feeling about what I've done," I said to Classius, my friend and comrade. I wondered if saying these words was wise, but for some reason, wisdom wasn't my foremost thought.

"Strange feeling?" he asked confused. "Like a sore arm?"

"No, nothing physical," I said shaking my head as we slowly walked through the streets of Jerusalem with our torches held high. The flickering flame wasn't very bright due to the wind and rain.

"Then no," he said flatly looking at a few barrels outside a home.

I stopped walking. I didn't know why I felt the need to stop, but my legs wouldn't budge. I had a nagging feeling in my heart that caused a lagging feeling in my legs.

"What's wrong?" he asked. "You know we have to get to Pilate's to find out our next orders soon. Maximus said he believes we are going to be guarding that Jesus' tomb. The Jews are afraid that some of his crazy followers are going to do something. You know how people lose their senses when they get cornered."

I nodded in agreement. We had seen it many times before when a loved one was executed. Their family or friends would try to make a scene, but that usually only ended up with them being imprisoned or worse, dead.

"I want to be one of the guards at his tomb," I said weakly. "I think." My tone came out with an air of uncertainty, but I was sure something beyond myself was beckoning me to stand guard for this man. I felt the need to watch over this Jewish man's tomb, a man I had never seen or met before in my life. I didn't even know why he was nicknamed King of the Jews, but the way he looked on the cross all beaten and bloody didn't look royal. He looked like a common criminal. A criminal despised and hated by everyone in the crowd.

"You think?" he laughed. "If you're ordered there, you don't have to think. You go."

"I know, I know," I said defending my allegiance and my duty. "But I'm thinking of requesting a shift or trading with someone if they get it and I don't."

"I don't think you'll have a hard time trading with anyone who gets the boring job of standing in front of the grave of a nobody," he snickered. "Who even cares about this man? So what if someone comes and steals his body? If his followers want it, let them have it."

"See, that's what I'm talking about," I agreed, looking into the window of a nearby home to see a family huddled around the table with bread and wine. "There has to be something else about this man."

"You're thinking too much," he laughed. "I've never seen you like this, Longinus."

"Longinus," a voice whispered nearby.

"Did you hear that?"

"Hear what?" Classius said unfazed. "All I hear is the wind at my back," he said looking around the darkened, deserted road. "Can we get moving? I'm wet, and I'm cold, and I'm ready to eat. It's been a long day and we have another long day tomorrow." Classius started walking ahead of me.

I took a deep breath and pushed my legs to take a step.

Chapter 17

Peter

"Longinus," I said with bated breath, quickly shutting my mouth once I realized I could be heard.

"Did you hear that?" Longinus asked.

He stood a few cubits away from where I was hiding. I peered my head around the barrels to see him. He stood statuesque like a Roman god with rippling muscles rolling out of his uniform from years of training and fighting. His torch highlighted the profile of his face. He had a large slanted nose and piercing blue eyes. His face was tan from years of working in the sun, and his hair was a sandy color with an occasional blond streak. I stared intently. I closed my eyes, but I could still see this man in my memory. He looked like any other Roman guard I had seen, but this one was different. This one killed my friend.

The thought of him pulling my friend's arms apart to nail a spike into his wrist sent a chill through my body. The man who probably spit in Jesus' face as they lifted up the splintered cross was within my reach.

I considered reaching out my hand and pulling him behind the barrels and attacking him. He wouldn't expect it, but I knew I couldn't fend off the other soldier.

But at least now I had a name and a face. I knew who my foe was.

"Hear what?" the other guard asked. "All I hear is the wind at my back. Can we get moving? I'm wet, and I'm cold, and I'm ready to eat. It's been a long day and we have another long day tomorrow."

The other guard started to walk away as Longinus stood still. He was so close I could hear him breathe.

An evil thought flashed.

I could kill him. The other guard walked away and I could flee before he would notice me. It was dark. It was rainy. It was foggy.

It could work.

I came up with a quick plan as Longinus took a step away from me. I started to see my opportunity begin to close, so I slowly stood up, rising behind the barrels. I left the comfort of being hidden and quietly snuck up behind the trailing guard. Tiptoeing behind, I was just two arm lengths' away. One quick jump and I could surprise and strangle him.

"Longinus," I whispered, hoping he would turn so I could jump on him and get him off balance.

He started to turn as I was about to attack.

"Longinus, are you coming?" the other guard asked, turning around to see his comrade.

I quickly darted into the shadow and pressed up against the wall. I held my breath to not make a sound.

"Coming," Longinus said trotting up to the other guard.

I watched as the two men walked side by side heading toward Pilate's home. On one side I hated to have this moment pass without doing anything, but on the other side, I was relieved I didn't hurry the process.

If he guarded Jesus' tomb, there would be another chance to kill him. And most likely, he would be alone.

I could come up with a well-devised plan to kill Longinus and get rid of the body before anyone would notice. In a day's time I could come up with the perfect act of revenge.

Maybe even get some help.

I walked slowly up the road, as my scattered thoughts ricocheted in every direction. One thought would instantly spur on three others, all going into different directions. My regret had been overtaken with another feeling. And this feeling was soon taking over all my thoughts and reasoning.

Revenge was a powerful thing.

Revenge was becoming an all-encompassing friend.

When I arrived at Mary's house, I knocked on the front door. I expected to see a friendly face, but all I saw was John.

"What do you want?"

Chapter 18

John

"What do you want?" I asked, annoyed at seeing Peter so soon after our disagreement. I was tempted to hit him again, but he immediately barged into the house.

He looked around the room filled with people who had stood beside me as we watched Jesus die. I hoped Peter felt guilt. I hoped he felt regret so deep he would toss and turn for many sleepless nights to come, and when he did fall asleep, I hoped nightmares of remorse would wake him. I hoped he realized when he deserted Jesus, he also deserted us.

He ran across the room and fell at Mary's feet.

"Mary, oh Mary," he started to tearfully plea. "I'm so sorry, Mary. I don't know why I…" he started when Mary placed a finger over his lips and shook her head.

I was waiting for her to tear into him. I watched with great anticipation, hoping to see her legs twitch to remove the life sucking leech off her feet. Her eyes stopped crying. Her demeanor changed from fragile to strong. This was the moment I had waited for.

"Peter," she said shaking her head as she continued to press her finger to his trembling lips. "Don't say another word."

The words caused my heart to leap for joy. She was shutting Peter up with just a touch of her hand and a look in her eyes.

He crumbled before her, but instead of scolding him, she warmly laid his head in her lap and started to lovingly caress his hair. "Oh,

Peter, I know," is all she said as soothingly and maternally as anyone would say to their frightened child.

My heart ceased its bounce for joy and crashed into the pit of despair.

"How can you say that?" I asked uncontrollably. "He left us alone!"

Mary looked up at me and shook her head. "But we're together now, John." She radiated love and mercy, but I wasn't ready for such forgiveness. I wanted to scorn the man who left us. I wanted to hurt the man who cared more about his own well-being than the protection of everyone else. In my book, Peter was a coward. A coward like the rest of them.

Peter looked around at me, wiping his eyes with his rugged hands. "John, I know I disgust you, but I promise you, I disgust myself much more than you could ever imagine. I know I don't deserve forgiveness, but I'm sorry, John."

I looked at Peter and I wanted to keep my fury. I wanted to nurture the hate I had for him and let it grow rampant. I knew if I just let it stew for a while, a forest of unforgiveness could grow high enough so I wouldn't have to look upon Peter ever again. But something from my recollection cut down the growing emotions.

I remembered a time when Peter had asked Jesus, "Lord, how often will my brother sin against me, and I forgive him? As many as seven times?"

Jesus had looked at him, "I do not say to you seven times, but seventy-seven times." Jesus continued answering in his storytelling ways and told us a tale of an unforgiving servant who begged for forgiveness from his master but never gave forgiveness to people who asked him for it. I remembered standing in front of Jesus as he told this parable and thinking it seemed so reasonable.

Jesus had continued, "Then his master summoned him and said to him, 'You wicked servant! I forgave you all that debt because you pleaded with me. And should not you have had mercy on your fellow servant, as I had mercy on you?' And in anger his master delivered him to the jailers, until he should pay all his debt. So also my heavenly Father will do to every one of you, if you do not forgive your brother from your heart."

My heart dropped. I wasn't ready to forgive the mistakes of those that have hurt me.

It was as if I could hear the words of Jesus speaking over me at that very moment. I looked down at Peter and knew what I needed to say, but I couldn't say it. I just couldn't. Listening to Jesus' teachings was always easier than actually doing them. He taught about loving everyone, and it seemed like a good principle as he was speaking. But at that moment I wasn't ready to love everyone. There were many people I wasn't sure I would ever be ready to love.

I leaned against the wall and turned my head so I couldn't see the group gathered in the room. A few of the people had left; Joseph and Nicodemus needed to return home to their families, and a few other women had entered. Peter was the first of my close knit group that had come to check on Mary.

But at least he had come. The other ten were still missing.

"I'm sorry," I heard Peter softly say as he approached my side. He leaned in for a hug, but I wasn't ready for that type of affection. I wasn't ready to be that close to him just yet.

"Not yet, Peter," I said, turning away from his embrace and walking to the other side of the room.

"This is not the time for division," Mary Magdalene said as she unclasped Mary's hand from hers. She shakily stood and walked towards Peter. "This is when we need each other the most," she said encouragingly as her eyes twinkled with new tears. "Especially now." She leaned and hugged Peter with a warm embrace. I watched from across the room as they looked into each other's eyes. They didn't say a word to each other, but their looks spoke for them.

There was forgiveness in her eyes.

There was healing in his.

Chapter 19

Mary Magdalene

"Especially now," I said reaching out to Peter to offer a compassionate hug. He gladly received the touch of affection. There was no judgment, no animosity, no strings attached in our actions. We were just two people leaning on one another during this difficult time. Sadly, there were going to be many more moments like this in the coming weeks.

"I should have been there with you all," he whispered in my ear, barely audible.

"It's okay," I whispered with my head against his strong, sturdy shoulder. "Mary's right," I said encouragingly. "You're here now."

We released each other, and I turned around to find John sulking on the other side of the room. I debated going to him and offering him the same shoulder to lean on, but something stopped me. He didn't want a friendly gesture and I knew no matter what I did or said, it wouldn't have done any good.

"Mary," I said, "you need to eat something. Let me fix it for you."

"No," she said shaking her head, "I can't eat anything right now."

I looked around the room to see if anyone else needed anything, but everyone sided with Mary. That was the thing about grief. It's easy to forget about everything else when in the middle of it.

"At least he didn't suffer as long as others have," Lydia, a friend of Mary's, said optimistically. I knew she meant well, and in times of silence people try to fill the gaps with words, but sometimes silence was better in moments like this.

I took my seat next to Mary, clutching her hand and allowing her to squeeze the anger into my fingers, but she didn't. She just nodded to Lydia.

Lydia opened her mouth to say something, but I quickly shot her a look of warning. She heeded my advice and closed her mouth. Technically, Lydia's words were correct. There had been some crucifixions that had lasted days. I hated to see someone suffer, especially in humiliation, so most of the time when I knew there was going to be one, I would do whatever I could to not go near Golgotha. Luckily, I lived further away from the hill than some people, so I never had to hear the poor soul wail through the night. Some sounds should never be heard.

I knew Lydia only meant the best. Mary and Lydia had been friends for more years than I could recall, but sometimes words said in an act of sympathy came out unintentionally hurtful.

"Does someone want to read the Passover passage?" Phoebe, another friend of Mary's, asked.

Various people looked around the room unsure of the answer. It was customary to read the holy story and partake in a feast on this evening, but tonight didn't feel like a night to remember how God saved the Hebrew children so many years earlier.

Tonight, we needed another Passover, a miracle, something that would cause all of this pain and torrid memories to pass over and not settle on our hearts and minds. I turned my head toward the table in the eating area and my heart stopped. I hadn't noticed it before.

On the middle of the table sat four cups with a stack of plates and a large bowl nearby. I looked around the room and noticed it was perfectly clean.

My heart broke a little more. Mary was prepared for the Passover feast. She had everything ready. As I looked straight ahead I found the basins by the door to wash the feet of the guests. The only thing missing was the meal that would have been prepared this evening with the unblemished male lamb as the sacrifice.

I had celebrated Passover every year of my life, but last year's meant more to me than any that had come before. It was the last one I would have with my friend and teacher, Jesus.

I looked around the room and realized many people in this room had been around during the last Passover feast. But many people were missing, and that saddened me to know they were grieving, afraid, and probably alone.

No one should be alone in moments like this. I unclasped my friend's hand and gave her a goodbye hug. "I'll be back, Mary," I said standing up to leave.

"Where are you going?" Peter asked as he started to follow me.

"To find the others," I softly said, trying to keep my words away from Mary's ears.

"The others?" John asked confusedly as he, too, followed me to the door. "Why?"

"Why not?" I asked, shrugging my shoulder and putting on my head garment to protect myself from the wind and rain.

"You can't go out there alone," Peter said.

Chapter 20
Peter

"You can't go out there alone," I said with concern coursing through my veins. "It's too late for you to be roaming the streets."

"I'm not afraid," Mary Magdalene said defiantly. "Are you?"

To be honest, I was afraid. I had been lurking in the alleyways, hiding my face from anyone who could possibly recognize me all day. I knew since they killed Jesus, they could also come after me if they wanted. Sadly, the shadows had been my friends today more than anyone else. It's a sad life living in the shadows. It was a sad day retreating to a safe house of denial.

"I'll go with you," John snidely said standing beside me. "*I'm* not afraid." He said those words as he looked squarely in my eyes so I could feel his judgment. He wanted me to know he wasn't afraid now or earlier today. But I knew it was an adolescent lie.

"Do you know where the others could be?" Mary Magdalene asked as she opened the door to leave Mary's house.

"No," John said shaking his head.

"I do," I answered unsurely.

"Peter," Mary Magdalene said sympathetically, "you don't have to go with us." She looked at me with mixed emotions. On one side she didn't want to force me to go, but on the other hand, I could tell she would beg me to lead her to the others.

"No," I said with a smile. I knew what I needed to do. "I'll go."

The three of us exited Mary's home and walked the deserted rainy streets of Jerusalem. As we walked I started to ignore the sound of the splashing rain. I could hear the excitement in the homes we were passing. Thousands of visitors had come to Jerusalem for Passover, so homes that usually had only a few people were filled with family and friends reconnecting, laughing, and enjoying each other's company as they reflected on the purpose of this night. The glorious night of Passover needed to be remembered and celebrated for generations to come.

"So, where are they?" John passively asked, walking behind me and Mary Magdalene.

"Shhh," I said, not wanting to cause commotion this late in the evening. "We will get there."

I could hear John huff in annoyance. He was the younger brother to James, and he was used to feeling inferior. But I had learned to overlook it, just as he had learned to overlook my flaws. After spending the last three years together traveling from village to village, I started to learn the idiosyncrasies of those I shared a mat with under the twinkling stars. I looked overhead, but I couldn't see any stars, just storm clouds covering the celestial lights.

"Remember that time…" I asked softly, forgetting that Mary Magdalene wasn't with us on that trip. "Oh, never mind, you weren't with us, Mary."

"Tell it anyways," she said. "I could use a good story."

"We were heading to Gerasenes. Jesus had taught all day and he'd wanted to take a boat across the sea. Suddenly, a powerful storm came out of nowhere and started to rock the boat. The waves were crashing over the railings, and I thought we were all going to die," I said still recalling the fear of being on the open waters without any way of escape. "Mary, the boat was sinking."

"What happened?" she asked.

"Jesus happened," John answered behind us. I stopped in shock as he patted me on the back in a friendly way telling me to continue walking. "I don't remember who woke Jesus up," he said as Mary interjected.

"Jesus was asleep as you were about to sink?"

"That he was," Peter smiled. "Right when he woke up -- I don't know how -- but it was like he was speaking to the storm, 'Peace! Be still!' was all he said and then suddenly the storm passed. The clouds parted, the sun came out, and there was no trace of a storm on the horizon. Even the puddles in the boat vanished just as quickly as they had formed."

"I heard someone else tell me something similar," Mary stated. "Remarkable."

"Very," John echoed.

"But..." Mary quietly said, shivering in realization.

"But what?" John asked.

"But he didn't do it today," she said feebly. She took a few steps and then turned to me. "Why didn't he do it today?"

I looked at her and saw the distraught look in her eyes. She was like a walking conundrum. One minute we could look back and delight in stories from the past when Jesus did the unbelievable, and in the next we could come back to here and now when Jesus did the unbelievable again. But this time the unbelievable was his death.

"I don't know," I answered in surrender. I couldn't come up with a plausible explanation for the events of the last week. Nothing made sense.

"He didn't even fight in the garden last night," John said softly. "He didn't even fight."

Chapter 21

John

"He didn't even fight in the garden last night," I said depressingly. "He didn't even fight." I stopped and looked up at the cloudy sky. "It's like he gave up or something."

I couldn't believe Jesus allowed the guards to take him down in the garden of Gethsemane without lifting a fist. He didn't stand his guard. He didn't command the scene. He just surrendered. I looked over at Peter, the coward, and gained a little more respect for the man as I remembered how he had lifted his sword and cut off Malchus' ear. I didn't even have the nerve to fight last night.

"Why did he give up?" I asked. I didn't know who I was asking, because Mary hadn't seen what I saw and I wasn't ready to have a discussion with Peter just yet. "He said he was going to rule a kingdom," I said optimistically, but as the words escaped my lips the positive tone dissolved into the midnight sky.

"I don't get it, John," Peter cautiously spoke. "We could have taken the guards. We outnumbered them."

"You even sliced one of their ears off!" I exclaimed.

"You did what?" Mary asked, stopping in her tracks and looking at Peter in confusion.

"You heard him right," Peter solemnly agreed. "When they came after Jesus, my gut instinct was to protect the group, so I grabbed my sword and swung."

"But they were guards," she said stunned. "You could have been arrested for that," she remarked like an older sister watching out for her careless little brother.

That's when it hit me. Peter did have a reason to hide. He was the only one of us that stood up to fight against the men who captured our friend. He was the only brave one. I didn't have an ounce of bravery in me last night.

Last night I was in a petrified state of shock, but Peter had the gumption to stand his ground. I looked over at Peter and a surge of remorse filled my insides. He had not only pulled out his sword to defend Jesus, but he had also defended me.

A silent tear began to roll down my cheek, and my nose started to run. I tried to stifle the sound of my sniff, but it seemed like it was louder than the thunder and howling wind.

"John," Peter said softly, "you okay?"

I couldn't speak. I didn't want to say anything because of how I had treated Peter just a few minutes ago. I wanted to hold onto the grudge like the stupid teenager I was, but I knew that wasn't the right thing to do now.

I wiped my nose on the arm of my robe and ignored his question.

"Then Jesus picked up the ear and healed it, Mary," I said mundanely. "He actually healed the man who had come with his captors."

"He healed him?" Mary asked in disbelief. "Maybe he didn't think he was going to be taken prisoner."

"He knew," I said, looking over at Peter. "He told Peter to put up his sword and then he said something strange: 'Shall I not drink the cup that the Father has given me?'"

"Drink the cup?" Mary asked confusedly. "What cup?"

"I don't know," I said shrugging my shoulders. "I felt dumb around Jesus a lot when he would teach. Sometimes I had no clue what he meant, but I didn't want to be the only one to look stupid, so I kept my questions to myself."

"You wouldn't have looked stupid, John," Peter encouraged. "I didn't understand him most of the time either," he commented with a disheartened tone. "And I was the oldest. I didn't want to look bad in front of you all, so I stayed silent too."

"I never said anything because I didn't want you to look down at me for being so young," I said wide-eyed. "I thought I had to prove something to the rest of you."

"Oh John," Peter smiled, shaking his head. "You never had to prove anything to us. Jesus loved you more than any of us."

"No he didn't," I scoffed at the absurdity of the statement. "He loved us all the same."

"He may have loved us all, but he loved you differently," Peter said, grasping my shoulder like a father figure. "Sometimes being the youngest has its advantage, so don't ever think you have to prove yourself to me."

My nose started to run again, but I quickly tried to stop it.

"I'm sorry, Peter," I softly said looking into where his eyes would be if I could see them.

"No, I'm sorry."

Chapter 22

Peter

"No, I'm sorry," I said placidly. "Sorry I wasn't there for you today." I looked over at where Mary was standing but could only see a shadowed figure. I couldn't see her judgmental eyes weighing heavily on me. Even if she wasn't judging me, I was. I may not have seen Mary's eyes at that moment, but I would never forget the eyes of the woman who had identified me earlier that day. I started to walk again, hoping I could leave the memory behind, but it followed me.

"This man was with him," the young woman had hissed, pointing me out in the middle of the crowd. She wasn't well off, probably a servant. She was likely overlooked by everyone, but for the first time in a long time, she was being heard.

Everyone had quickly turned their head in my direction. I felt the world cave in and start to spin wildly. Men were shouting, but I couldn't hear what they were saying. I quickly found myself in the middle of a whirlpool of fear and doubt. I spun around blurring all the faces, all but hers.

Her face pierced my soul; it was the only thing I could clearly see. Her image was my focal point, her tattered gown with unraveled edges around her ankles from wear and tear through the years. She had probably been wearing that dress for years and had finally grown tall enough so it didn't trip her as she walked. Her veil wasn't anything impressive with a few holes throughout, probably from where the wind blew the covering into a thorn bush and the fabric snagged as she'd pulled it loose.

Before today she would not have been noticed. But today, she had something to say.

"Woman, I do not know him," I quickly defended, but it was too late. I could already smell the anger on everyone's breath. Somehow I fled the scene. A few followed me, but I darted through alleyways until I had lost the last straggler.

Then it happened twice more.

"He told me I would do it," I mumbled to myself.

"What did you say, Peter?" Mary asked compassionately.

"He warned me," I softly answered, turning down the same deserted alley I had hid in earlier that day.

"Warned you about what? About this?" John asked.

"But I didn't believe him," I said, tuning out their questions. "I told him that I wouldn't."

"Peter, what are you talking about?"

I remembered Jesus saying to me, "Where I am going you cannot follow me now, but you will follow afterward." He had spoken gently and compassionately, as if consoling me.

"Lord, why can I not follow you now? I will lay down my life for you," I had answered. At least, I'd thought I could do it. But words are easier than actions, and he knew that. He always knew.

"Will you lay down your life for me?" he'd asked me, looking into my eyes and seeing the truth. "Truly, truly, I say to you, the rooster will not crow till you have denied me three times," he had said with a disheartened smile. It was a smile given to someone who was blinded to their own shortcomings as I was to mine.

In a matter of time he was correct.

80

One.

Two.

Three.

The rooster crowed.

"The rooster crowed," I stammered incoherently. "After the third time, it crowed like he said it would."

"Peter," John said, grabbing my shoulder to stop me, "you're scaring me."

"It's scaring me too," I said looking at the dark, narrow passageway between two homes. "We are here."

"Isn't this…" John started to ask before I nodded my head.

Chapter 23

John

"Isn't this where we were last night?" I asked vaguely seeing Peter's head bob up and down as he proceeded down the darkened alleyway.

"Wait a minute," Mary said timidly. "This is where you gathered last night?"

The three of us stood in the darkened alley. I thought outside was bleak, but upstairs was uncertain. I couldn't see Peter leading the way as he walked through the secret passageway easily ignored by anyone passing by. I felt his hand reach for me, patting my elbow down to my wrist and grabbing hold to direct me. I did the same for Mary.

We didn't talk as we made our short journey. I felt like an intruder, much different than last night. Last night, the thirteen of us were laughing and sharing stories as we walked this little alleyway, but not tonight. Tonight we were deathly quiet.

Peter found his way to the stairs. The creak of the first one told Mary and I we were heading up. I didn't recall hearing the creaking steps last night, but once again, we were not in fearful silence last night. It seemed like silence also rattled my nerves. The night was when I felt defenseless or easily victimized. It was always in the night when horror tales crept into my mind and I started to see the ghostly images. It was always in the dark when fear seemed greater than myself. Always in the dark.

I pressed my body against the wall, blending into the shadow. I looked around and I could see the surrounding homes as I climbed higher off the ground. A fear hit me. If I could see them, could they see me? But my fear subsided as I looked behind and could barely make out Mary's features.

We slowly trekked up the aging staircase that moaned in agony with the weight of our bodies on its frame. We still didn't say a word. Then it hit me, this wasn't the second time I had walked up the steps with Peter, but the third.

Yesterday, the thirteen of us were out in the countryside and Jesus had approached me and Peter. "Go and prepare the Passover for us, that we may eat it," Jesus said.

"Where will you have us prepare it?" I didn't ask too many questions in front of the group, but since Jesus pulled me aside, I felt more compelled. I didn't feel like a fool.

"Behold, when you have entered the city, a man carrying a jar of water will meet you. Follow him into the house that he enters and tell the master of the house, 'The teacher says to you, where is the guest room where I may eat the Passover with my disciples?' And he will show you a large upper room furnished; prepare it there."

We had followed his instructions and found the man carrying a clay pot filled to the brim with water. We'd startled him as we approached, and as he turned a large wave of water splashed onto my robe. He was surprised when we said what Jesus told us, yet something in his eyes let us know he wasn't shocked. It was like he knew.

I remembered walking through his warm, hospitable house as the windows let in the light from the outside. He got a handful of candles and shook his head as if somewhat confused. He turned and looked at me with a quizzical expression but didn't say a word, even though I could tell he wanted to say something. He shook his head as if erasing his thought and then led us to the little passageway beside his home. We didn't need a candle to walk up the stairs then; the light from the sun led the way. As we entered the room, it was as Jesus had said. He had all the furnishings for Passover.

"Did the teacher approach you earlier?" I asked.

He shook his head no and scratched his head in thought.

"Do you always have extra in case someone asks to use this upper room?" I asked again.

He once again shook his head no. He opened his mouth and then stopped. He looked at me with confusion as if he had something to say, but didn't know how to say it. I just smiled kindly because I had often been speechless around Jesus.

He shrugged his shoulders and started to speak. "It was my wife," he smiled. "She said for me to get the room ready tonight. She felt it was going to be needed."

"Your wife?" I asked shocked. "So, could she have talked with Jesus recently?"

He started to smile as his eyes started to fill with tears. "Oh, son, you wouldn't believe me if I told you," he said and started to walk away.

Chapter 24

Benjamin

"Oh, son, you wouldn't believe me if I told you," I said laying the candles on the table as I turned to leave this sacred room.

"No, we will believe you," John said as Peter nodded in agreement.

I looked uneasily around the room, seeing the work I had done in the last week for this moment. I had thought was a stupid idea, but I'd wanted to adhere to my wife's plea.

Suddenly, it was as if I was taken back eleven months earlier, standing here in this room with my wife, lying fragile on her bed.

"Come here, Benjamin," she coughed out with tired eyes that had aged through the last few months of fight.

"What, my love?" I had asked, leaning down and stroking her shimmering gray hair. I always called her *my love*. We had lived a long life together and she was always my love.

"For Passover, use this room," she strained to say. "Have this room ready for Passover."

I smiled down at her. I didn't want her to feel uncomfortable in her last moments. I didn't want to confuse or upset her. I wanted my love to just keep talking to me like nothing else was happening.

"Really, Benjamin, someone will be asking to use this room," she said as she reclined. "I can see it now," she smiled as her eyes lit up. "The world is going to change."

"Yes, my love," I nodded, listening to every word she spoke as if she was whispering sweet nothings like we were newly married again.

"Oh, Benjamin," she said with a playful smile. "I can tell you don't believe me. I may be dying, but I'm still here," she said pointing up at her head. "I am still all right here."

"I know, my love. I know you are still here," I sniffled, thinking that soon she wasn't going to be right here. Passover had just happened a month ago and we were alone, and now she was planning for the next Passover and wanted to prepare for many people. A tear started to creep down my cheek as I watched the lucidness in her words fade. The physician had warned me this would happen.

She'd closed her eyes, smiled, and said, "It's going to be an incredible night."

I woke from my trance and saw these two unfamiliar guests staring at me. "Always do as your wife says," I kidded. "They are always right."

"We will, sir," the older one said as he once again thanked me for allowing them to use the upper room. The teenage boy started opening the contents on the table and found the herbs and spices for the meal. The room started to smell like Passover once again.

"I will let you be," I said starting towards the entryway. I turned and watched the room transform from what was once a sickbed room to a lively one.

"Where are…" the older one started to ask the younger as I left them to do their duty and prepare for their feast.

Chapter 25
Peter

"Where are…" I started to say but stopped myself. I remembered asking the same question of John the previous day, but now a feeling of uncertainty rose in my being. An uneasiness crept from deep in my soul. I clamped down on John's wrist as if telling him that I was still there, even though he knew. I needed some assurance that my hands were not numb and he and Mary hadn't run off.

In my mind, I was on the top step and found the upper room as we had left it last night. I closed my eyes and envisioned us reclining around the table, basking in the reason for our celebration. Suddenly, the night had switched from celebratory to dramatically serious. The first cup had been filled and the washing of hands had taken place. Jesus had brought out the bowl of red wine vinegar. We all knew that this symbolized the betrayal of Joseph in Genesis when his brothers dipped his beloved coat into the blood to convince their father that Joseph was killed. It is a brutal act of betrayal when brother betrays brother.

"Truly, I say to you, one of you will betray me," Jesus said looking into the distance. I had felt the mood change and his smile faded. He wasn't teaching us to love and protect one another anymore. He was charging one us with the unthinkable.

I'd nodded to John who had been reclining beside Jesus to ask the hard question. Jesus always had a soft place in his heart for John.

"Lord, who is it?" John had asked timidly with dry breath, his words cracking under the pressure.

Jesus hadn't answered immediately but carried on with the Passover meal. He went through the telling of the Passover like my father had for me for twenty years. Jesus came to the point in the ritual of dipping the vegetable into the bowl. As I dipped my item, I looked up at Jesus. "Is it I, Lord?"

But he didn't answer. A fear swept through me. I felt that I could never betray Jesus like Joseph's brothers, but as I looked around the room, I wondered if Reuben had had the same thought many years ago.

We each took turns dipping our item into the bowl. As the final one dipped his hand, Jesus also dipped his and swirled the bowl's contents so they commingled.

"He who has dipped his hand in the dish with me will betray me. The Son of Man goes as it is written of him, but woe to that man by whom the Son of Man is betrayed! It would have been better for that man if he had not been born," Jesus solemnly said as he looked into Judas' eyes.

"Is it I, Rabbi?" Judas asked as he scanned the room. All eyes were on Judas in shock and confusion.

I shook my head no, thinking that Judas couldn't possibly be the betrayer; he was our treasurer. We trusted him with our lives and our possessions. He definitely wouldn't be the betrayer or Jesus wouldn't have let him hold our money. He would have known Judas' true character. We all would, wouldn't we?

"You have said so," Jesus said. "What you are going to do, do quickly."

Judas had quickly left with the money bag. I had immediately thought Jesus must have told him to go buy more supplies because I didn't want to believe my friend and brother was going to betray Jesus.

And here I was the next day, just as confused. "Where is everyone?" I asked out loud as I walked into the dark and empty room. No one was inside. No one greeted us with a hug. It was deathly quiet.

"I thought they were going to be here," John questioned.

"I did too," I responded turning my back to the room to look at Mary and John.

I bowed my head in sadness as Mary shrieked. I looked up and saw the fear in her eyes but before I could do anything I felt the attack.

"Stop!"

Chapter 26

Mary Magdalene

"Stop!" I screamed as I saw the shadows along the wall move and jump in our direction. My mind went to three options: flee, cower, or fight. I knew I could leave Peter and John since I was the last one up the stairs and my left foot was still on a stair, but I couldn't leave them. "It's a trap!"

One figure collided with Peter, who didn't see it coming since he had his back to the person. His body slammed into the wall and I heard him groan, not in pain, but in anger.

John let go of my hand and ran into the room to grab the attacker. He jumped on the person's back and wrapped his bony arms around his neck and hung onto him as if riding a crazed ram.

"Peter!" John shouted as I moved closer to the wall, camouflaging myself in the dark room.

Peter didn't respond but grunted as he put up his fists to fight.

Suddenly, from the corner I saw another figure come running toward the three fighting men.

"John!" I screamed. "Behind you!" But it was too late; the moment I said the words the person had already yanked John from the first attacker's back and had him pinned to the floor.

"Run, Mary!" John yelled. "Run!"

"Mary?" another voice said from the room. "Peter? John? Is that really you?" the voice asked shakily.

"Who's there?" I pleaded. "Who are you?"

"Run, Mary!" Peter resounded as he threw another punch. "Don't trust them!"

"No!" the man shouted stepping away from the wall. Once again, all I could see was a shadowed figure walking closer to me.

"Stop! Stop right there!" I shouted, straightening my stature in case I needed to defend myself. I had never fought with anyone, but I wasn't going to go down without a fight. "Who are you?"

"Thomas," the man said boldly as he rushed to Mary's side. He reached up, felt my cheek, and hugged me. "It's really you," he said. "It's them!" he shouted as the two other attackers stopped fighting. "It's really them."

I looked keenly into the darkness, and suddenly a sliver of light came through the window and landed on the eyes of Thomas. It really was him. It was Thomas! I ended our hug and looked over at the other two figures as one helped John up from the floor and the other hugged Peter as if it was a joyous reunion of the ages.

I squinted my eyes to see the faces of the other two when suddenly more figures appeared out of the darkness. Suddenly I saw about a dozen figures standing in the room. My heart stopped with a thought, *Trust or fight?*

Was this a ploy to get more of Jesus' followers? To disarm them and crucify them just like they did to Jesus? I wasn't ready to trust just yet. I wasn't ready to lower my guard. I wasn't ready to watch more of my friends die.

"Who are you all?" I asked as fear started to pique. One by one they started to say who they were.

"James," a different voice answered.

"Andrew," one voice coughed out.

"Bartholomew."

"Phillip."

"Matthew," the one hugging Peter answered as I could finally start to recognize some of his features in the brief moonlight.

"James," the other James replied.

"Simon."

"Thaddaeus."

I felt a wave of peace rush over me. It was a sweet relief after the last two minutes of adrenaline-fueled fear.

Chapter 27

Thaddaeus

"Thaddaeus," I said, being the last one in the group to step out and answer. I had been hidden with my band of brothers for the last day. We could hear the shouts from the people watching the crucifixion. We heard their cheers and jeers at the criminals' expense. We hoped that Jesus wasn't one of the men executed today, but when we heard them chanting to release Barabbas, we knew that leaving this room wasn't an option. We were safe in this hidden upper room for the time being.

The various men walked up to Peter, John, and Mary and hugged them as if seeing them for the first time in a long time, but the last twenty-four hours had seemed longer than a day.

"Can we light a candle?" Mary asked, feeling around the walls, hoping not to bump or fall over anything hidden in the dark.

"No!" Thomas whispered. "We mustn't draw any attention to ourselves or they will find us."

"But…" she started to say as Peter walked over to her and grabbed her hand.

"Not yet, Mary," he kindly whispered in her ear. "Not just yet."

"So, it's true?" Matthew asked shakily. "He really is…" he stopped himself from saying the words.

"Dead?" John spoke up, as a little anger started to rise in his voice. "Yes, he's dead. You would have known that if you weren't thinking only about your safety. Do you know what Mary and the rest are going through?" He started to shake in fury. "No! No, you don't, because you didn't even have the guts to see her! You are just a bunch of cowards!" he continued in his rant.

"John," Peter said, trying to control him by placing his hands on his shoulders.

"Don't, Peter," he retorted. "Not right now!" He shook off the touch as the group of men listened to his speech. "I used to look up to each one of you, but right when I needed you the most, you were long gone!" He stopped and took a breath. "You were each gone!" He started to weep as he rushed out of the room and sat on the top step to get away from everyone.

"He did the same to me," Peter said softly to the group of disciples.

"You?" I asked in shock since Peter was the oldest. I thought if anyone would be there to defend our leader, Peter would have been. Peter just nodded his head.

"That little boy out there is braver than any one of us," Peter started. When a few of the men started to clamor, he added, "Just let me finish. We may each have had reasons for not showing up for our friend, and I know I regret it, but we have to face the facts. We scattered just like he said we would."

I closed my eyes and shook my head. Peter was right as my mind flashed to a scene last night.

We had just finished the early Passover meal and sung a song. A few continued to sing as we left the upper room and walked down the steps and made our way to the Mount of Olives. Jesus always liked to get away to places of seclusion to pray and meditate so he wouldn't be bothered. As we were standing around Jesus said, "You will all fall away because of me this night. For it is written, 'I will strike the shepherd and the sheep of the flock will be scattered.' But after I am raised up, I will go before you to Galilee."

In the last twenty-four hours I had been so focused on surviving that I had forgotten what Jesus said.

"He did warn us," I said looking around the group, realizing we had all fallen away from our beloved teacher and friend. "And yet we did nothing."

"Mary, go check on John," Peter said as he asked the rest of us to circle around him.

Chapter 28

Peter

"Mary, go check on John," I said bringing the rest of my friends and brothers around. "Thaddaeus, you said, 'And we did nothing.'"

"Yes," Thaddaeus answered, nodding his head.

"But what if we do something now?" I said with a plan I had been plotting for the last few hours.

"Do what?" Phillip inquired.

"Revenge," I said with a forceful tone. "Jesus was killed and we did nothing, but it's not over! No, it's far from over!"

"What can we do?" Simon asked. "We're not skilled soldiers, and who do you plan to get revenge on? The whole city was against Jesus. No one stood up for him."

"Maybe they were scared too," Peter answered with conviction. "There were many other people like us out there hunkering in the darkness tonight because they were too afraid to do something today. They knew the truth of who Jesus was. And yet they did nothing. They are just like us," I said gaining momentum as the words started to course through my veins like my life depended on it. "If we are feeling like this, I bet there are others. And if we do something to show the Council and the Roman guards who we are, I can guarantee more people will join our agenda. We may just be a dozen young men, but we have something they don't have. The truth of who Jesus was! He was an innocent man who died for no other reason than their fear of him. And if we don't do something quickly, they will start to pick us off one by one."

"You think that?" Bartholomew asked, swallowing hard.

"I don't just think it, I can guarantee it!" I said clutching my fist. "The guards are not going to just stand by and do nothing. If they killed Jesus without any proof, they will come after us as well."

"We just need to leave then," Thomas said. "If we do what you say, there are always going to be more guards to come and take the place of the ones we get, but there will not always be people to take our place once they get us."

"Thomas, what did Jesus tell us so many times before? With faith the impossible can happen. Jesus did the impossible many times. It's our time to show them what he was made of."

"But what if he wasn't?" Thomas faintly asked in remorse.

"What? What was that?" I asked again, disbelieving my ears after everything Thomas had seen Jesus do in the last three years.

"What if he couldn't do all the impossible things we believed he could do? If he could, wouldn't he be alive now?" Thomas stopped and lowered his head in disgust for thinking the words. "I'm sorry, Peter, but what if Jesus wasn't who we thought him to be? What if he was just a good teacher who was looking for some people to follow him?"

"You stop that, now, Thomas! Stop it!" I shouted as the group of men started to hush me to keep my voice low.

"Peter, it's late and people could come find us," Thaddaeus whispered. "Please, just lower your voice and we can talk about this later. Maybe we need a moment to just be."

"Just be?" I asked annoyed. "Be what? Pawns in their endgame? Another body to hang on a cross? Another example of treatment for disobedience to Rome? What do you mean, Thaddaeus?"

"I think you know what I mean, Peter," Thaddaeus said patting my shoulder as he walked out of the room to find Mary and John.

"Are the rest of you against me?" I huffed. "I thought we were in this together? Were the last three years for nothing?" I asked walking toward the window, watching the moon come and go between the moving clouds. "For nothing?"

I looked out the window and strained my eyes to see far off into the distance. I could see the lights shining from where the palace stood. I didn't want to stay cooped up for the rest of my life. I didn't want to have to watch my back for possible threats or a life sentence. I didn't want to roll over and let them rule my life.

"We hear you, Peter," Thomas said walking up and patting my back, but I quickly moved. I didn't feel like being touched by him at this moment.

Chapter 29

Thomas

"We hear you, Peter," I said leaving the pack in the middle and approaching Peter singled out by the window. I wanted him to know that I commiserated with him in this. He wasn't alone. I stuck my hand out and tried to pat his back, but he quickly shrugged it off. "Peter! Don't push me away."

"Push you away? You're the one walking away freely from all of us!" he shouted in my face. "It's not me pushing you away. You're doing it yourself."

I couldn't believe my ears. I was the one who walked over to Peter. It wasn't the other way around. "Peter, look at me!" I said agitatedly, but he didn't turn his head. "Look at me!" Once again he didn't even acknowledge my words. I grabbed his shoulder and twisted his body so we were face to face.

"Get your hands off me!" he barked. "Just don't."

"You haven't questioned anything that has happened in the last day?" I asked flatly. "Because I don't buy that one bit." I said stomping away. "Everyone in here has questioned what happened over the last three years, and for you to say you are above us. That you are better than us. That you are the wisest. Well, I don't even know you then."

"Just stop it, Thomas," Matthew said, stepping between me and Peter. He stood in the center, not leaning more toward either of us. "Just stop."

"Yeah, Thomas, listen to your boy, Matthew," Peter snidely remarked.

I shook my head at the ego I was seeing in Peter. An ego that others had mentioned before, but I had overlooked in my naivety. "Fine Peter, you're right as always. But you left Jesus just like the rest of us, so don't get all high and mighty now."

"And what does that mean?" Peter asked, whipping around so he could look in my direction.

"Just because you're the oldest doesn't mean you can talk to us like little boys," I snapped back. "You're not that much older than us."

"I'm old enough to know what I know," he muttered through clenched teeth.

"And what is that?" I asked, brushing past Matthew and stepping closer to Peter until only inches were between us. "Oh wise Peter, tell us what you know. Enlighten our feeble minds with your insight."

"I don't have to stand around here," Peter said as he walked through the room and bumped into a few of his friends.

"Where are you going?" John asked wiping his face as he met Peter in the doorway.

"I just need to leave," he said disgruntled.

"We just got here," Mary spoke up as she looked around the room and remembered these were the people they had walked through the night to find. "You need to stay."

"Just let me go," Peter said forcefully.

"Yeah, just let him go!" I shouted from across the room. "Let him leave like he was destined to do."

He stopped in his tracks. "We came looking for you. Remember that, Thomas. We came looking for you. We were worried about you all."

"Then stay," Matthew said encouragingly. "Let's just take a few breaths and then we can discuss your plan, Peter. I think it just took us off guard."

"Plan? What plan?" Mary asked Peter. When he didn't answer she looked around the room and asked again, "What plan?"

Chapter 30

Mary Magdalene

"What plan?" I asked again, and I could tell by the shuffling of feet around the room and the downcast heads that everyone knew of a plan. Everyone but me.

"It doesn't pertain to you, Mary," Peter said distantly, as if I wasn't a friend or follower. He was speaking to me as if I was a commoner.

"John, what plan are they talking about?" I asked, whispering into his ear, but he shrugged his shoulders.

"I was out there with you when all this happened," he answered, clueless as well.

"Peter wants us to..." Thomas started before one of the others stopped him from finishing his sentence.

"He doesn't want her to know," someone said, but I couldn't tell who spoke.

"So, that's how it's going to be?" I asked amazed. "I'm just a woman not allowed to know the men's business," I said shaking my head at the sexism displayed. "In less than a day I am back to being looked at as a piece of property and not a person. It took less than a day for all of Jesus' teachings to vanish from your minds. He called me daughter. I'm fearful of what you men will call me now," I said turning to leave the room.

"Mary, wait," Peter said, grabbing my arm before I could leave.

I stopped and tried to look him in his eyes, but Peter darted his eyes around the room, not giving me direct contact.

"Have something to say, Peter?"

"You are right," he resigned, finally looking at me. "You are an equal to us."

"So tell me," I asked unrelentingly. "Just tell me the plan."

"We haven't decided anything," Thomas spoke up from across the room. "We were going to talk more later."

Peter turned his head to locate Thomas in the darkness. I couldn't see their faces, but I knew an apology and forgiveness was found somewhere in the middle. "Yeah, we were going to talk about it later."

"I can wait for later," I said as I walked into the center of the room, found a few of my friends, and gave them a gentle hug and kiss on the cheek. "How have you been?"

One by one they started to tell me their stories of heartbreak and agony. One by one they shared their concerns and their doubts, and I nodded in agreement with each. They shared their fears and distrust. But mostly they wondered about their future.

"What do we do now?" James asked solemnly.

Chapter 31

James – The Brother of John

"What do we do now?" I asked Mary and the rest of the group. No one said a word. No one knew what the future held or even wanted to know what was going to come.

"I mean, I left my father and his business three years ago to come follow Jesus," I said, remembering myself three years younger rocking in the boat with my father Zebedee and my younger brother John off the coast in the Sea of Galilee. I had been mending the nets after a long day of fishing. My father was counting the catch of the day and figuring if we needed to work anymore or call it a day.

I remember looking up with the nets in my hand and seeing two fellow sailors walking along the shoreline with an older man whom I had seen in temple and around the city but did not know personally. I knew a little about Peter and Andrew. I knew they were brothers like me and John. Peter and I had something in common in that we were both the older brother. We were always friendly with head nods or greetings each morning as we got into separate boats for a day of work, but beyond that, they were our competition. Fish that they caught were fish we couldn't catch. At the end of the day, we had a livelihood to maintain for our family.

Our father was a great fisherman. He had taught me and my brother everything we knew. He had been taking us on his fishing trips for many years, but at that moment, we had to decide to either follow in his footsteps or take a different path of following a rabbi.

"Follow me, and I will make you fishers of men," Jesus had said to me and John. I knew whatever I decided, John would do the same. He always followed in my footsteps. I looked at my father and he'd said it was my decision, but I could tell in his eyes he wanted me to follow him and take up the family business. I'd shown complete loyalty to my father during my sixteen years, but something in Jesus' voice was igniting a spark inside me that fishing never stirred.

"Father, please don't be upset," I had said to him.

"Upset?" he'd asked putting on a brave face. "How could I be upset with you, James? But John, you're going to stay with your Papa, right?"

I'd felt the chasm I had put my brother in, but I knew no matter what Father said to him, he was going to follow me. "You don't have to follow me, John. It's your decision," I'd stated, looking at John and then my father.

"I'm sorry, Papa, but I need to go too," John said as we paddled the boat to the shore.

We had both waved farewell to our father, but he had quickly gone back to tending his nets. I never fully knew if he was disappointed with me. I didn't know which thought was worse, his indifference when I left to follow Jesus or his sadness when John followed as well.

Returning to the present, I asked, "I mean, do I need to go back to my father's business and start over as a fisherman? Is that going to be my life now? Will my father even take me back?" I looked around at the group of followers and I saw their eyes widen. Each one had a similar decision to make. Jesus had cared for and provided for us for the last three years. Who was going to provide for us now?

"You can worry about that later," Mary kindly said as she leaned over and squeezed my hand. "That's for another day."

"But when?" I asked befuddled. "I spent the last three years following Jesus, but now that he is gone…" I stopped and hated to continue, but it was a question I had to ask. "When do I start again? Do I just pretend like the three years didn't happen? Do I go back to my father with my tail between my legs and ask for forgiveness for leaving him three years ago and following a man that led me right back to where I had begun?" I looked over and saw my little brother and a well of emotions surged up.

"I'm sorry, John," I said with a stifled cry. "I knew when I followed Jesus, you were going to follow. I'm sorry I led you down this bad path."

"Don't say that, James," he said compassionately. "It was my decision to follow, not yours."

"But I knew," I said with a deep breath. "I knew my decision would be yours as well." I stopped and looked over at him. "Not all big brothers make the right choices."

"I never said you made a wrong one," John corrected with a warm smile that filled the emptiness of my heart. He always had a way of seeing the good in every situation. It was his gift. Some called it his young blind eyes, but his eyes saw more than most. He saw the unlimited possibilities of the world we could never see. "You have always been the best brother, James. Always."

Those words meant everything to me. Even after I fled last night for my safety, I wasn't thinking about John's well-being. Yet, he didn't even notice my flight instincts for survival. Once again, he saw the possibilities of me. Possibilities that I couldn't see in myself. All I saw was a washed-up has-been who would have to beg for a mat to sleep on in my father's house. I would have to swallow my pride. Sadly, I might have to use John's favoritism for my benefit in order to get back in my father's good graces. He might have turned me away, but he would never turn his youngest son away.

Never.

"I can't go back to tax collecting either," Matthew said depressingly. "I won't."

Chapter 32
Matthew

"I can't go back to tax collecting either," I said quietly. "I won't."
I was hated and despised by everyone, including my friends and family,
unless I gave them a portion of what I swindled. I connived them into
thinking I was being fair to them when I collected their dues. They
should have known I was just a crook behind a stand. But sadly, they
never expected it from me. Whatever I gave to them, I just took back
eventually, with a little more to keep in my pocket. It was a cycle. One
in which I always came out ahead.

I looked around the room and saw my friends, each with
undesirable pasts. We all had histories that would not be held highly in
elitist social circles. We would all be looked down on as if we were
nothing but dirty shepherds or slaves. We may not have had a good
reputation three years ago as all the other rabbis overlooked us in their
choosing, but our recognition grew.

I used to think it was a good thing, but now I saw it may just be a
target on our backs. I didn't know what to think. On one side I felt
safe and comfortable, knowing I had true friends around me tonight,
closer to me than a brother. On the other hand, I felt I could be easily
betrayed and abandoned like we left Jesus last night.

I left a man who had singled me out when no one would give me
a second chance, but he saw something in me I couldn't see in myself.

"Follow me," Jesus had calmly stated years ago as he'd
approached my tax booth.

I'd been astonished with the audacity in his words and approach. He hadn't tried to sell himself with a grand charade or smoke and mirrors. He hadn't tried to mesmerize me with flashy lights and catchy hooks. He hadn't tried to win me over with false hopes and lofty promises. He'd merely said, "Follow me."

At the time, I thought it was stupid for me to waste one second of thought considering his proposition, but soon that second turned into a minute. In that minute I weighed the pros and cons. I had a choice of living life as a con artist or starting a clean slate with limitless potential. He didn't say he was going to wow me or even bargain with me to give him a week to see a change. He'd just said, "Follow me."

I didn't remember what caused me to leave my booth. I could not retrace my thoughts to find what sparked the change in my heart to give up my wealth to follow a penniless carpenter without a mass following. I could guarantee more people knew my name as a young, ruthless, tax collector than the name of Jesus. Too many. Jesus was just a man who wanted a change.

And I had wanted a change too.

So I'd left my booth and did as he asked. I followed him.

I had invited Jesus back to my house and asked him to join some of my colleagues for supper one last time. I had a nervous energy welling inside my bones. I had this unfamiliar excitement. I was on top of the world, even though my friends were laughing at my expense for tossing it all aside, but Jesus never wavered. He never let up. He continued to speak words of hope and forgiveness. I didn't know if he knew those were the things I was battling the most in my early career.

My family was upset with me when I became a tax collector because they thought I would follow my father's occupation, but I knew there was more money to be had in tax collecting. In Jewish culture, I might as well have disowned my family to turn my back on my heritage and work for the Roman government. But I was young. I was foolish. I saw easy money and I didn't want to labor in vain like my father. I didn't want to work from sun up to sun down and barely make enough to support a family.

I wanted more. I wanted a lot more. To be fifteen and have someone offer me a job making more in a week than many people made in a month, who could pass that by? Well, most people in my town, but not me. So, I worked a couple of years and was climbing the ladder when Jesus stopped by.

I remember some people came by and started insulting me and my friends. I would never forget how humiliated I was when the men I looked up to in my youth were degrading me like a dog.

"Why do you eat and drink with tax collectors and sinners?" they asked Jesus.

I had felt ashamed and wanted to hide my face in disgrace. I immediately thought I had just ruined my life. I had just quit my job and my livelihood and now this rabbi I was going to follow was going to wake up from his delusion and realize I wasn't who he thought I was.

I was just as they called me, a tax collector and a sinner.

But Jesus hadn't agreed with their slurs. He hadn't quickly jumped up and run out of my house to get the shame off of his robe. He hadn't looked at me with pity.

"Those who are well have no need of a physician, but those who are sick. I have not come to call the righteous but sinners to repentance," he said with kindness as he wrapped his arms around my back, as if telling me, *Look up, Matthew. Look up. This is not who you are.*

The slanderers quickly left and Jesus sat around and laughed the rest of the night with my friends. That was just the first of many nights when Jesus would sit with a group of my friends and laugh and tell stories through the night. My circle of friends might have changed, but the laughs never did.

Returning to the present, I looked over at my circle of friends for the last three years and a smile landed on my face. "Do any of you remember when Jesus asked Peter to go fishing to pay for their taxes and Peter found a shekel in the fish's mouth?" I started to laugh recalling the looks on the tax collector's face when a coin fell from its flapping jaw. "The looks on their faces when Peter handed them the coin."

"Looks on *their* faces?" Peter joined in from the window. "I was dumbstruck myself," he said starting to laugh. "Of all places to find some money; yet, he knew."

"He always knew," I said with a grin. "He always knew."

"What made you think of that?" Andrew asked, sitting across the room in the same spot he was sitting last night. "Ready to get back to tax collecting?"

Chapter 33

Andrew

"What made you think of that?" I asked, looking behind me to see if my older brother Peter was still looking out the window. "Ready to get back to tax collecting?"

"Not quite," Matthew answered, shaking his head as he took a seat on the ground.

I hated to see Peter looking so distraught. He was the epitome of strength. Besides my father, he was the one who always looked out for me. He taught me how to fish, cast nets, and steer the boat during a storm. He even jumped into the water and saved my life when I tripped after getting caught in the ropes. He was always watching my back. Now I guess it was my turn to watch his.

As I stared at him, a chill went down my spine. We were in this room less than a day ago. How quickly things had changed. We were sitting in the dark, huddled together for some form of comfort. Last night we had candles illuminating the room; we were able to see each other's face. But tonight, tonight we could only remember what each other looked like.

Peter shuffled his feet, knocking something over. I watched as he bent down and rose with something in his hands. I squinted to see the object he was holding. It was the basin Jesus used to wash each of our feet last night.

"What I am doing you do not understand now, but afterward you will understand," Jesus had said as he bent down and started removing the embedded dirt from a day of traveling. He'd started with me.

"Andrew," he'd said as he poured the tepid water over my feet. "Remember when we first met?"

"I do," I had said feebly, trying to stifle a laugh as his hands started tickling the bottom of my feet. "I do."

"I remember it well too," he smiled as he looked up into my eyes. Instantly, it was as if it was just the two of us in the room. Jesus always had an uncanny way of making me feel like I was the center of his attention. It was like the rest of the world faded away and it was just the two of us. "You were fishing and I heard your laugh from the shore. Don't ever lose that joy, Andrew. The world needs to see that joy."

"I won't, Jesus." He continued to tell multiple stories centered on me. The moments when I made him proud. The times when I showed the potential he knew I had. The times when I stepped out in faith and trusted God had something bigger in store. It was as if he spoke to me for hours. He then wiped my feet dry. But before he moved on to the next person he asked me a question.

"Do you understand what I have done to you?" His smile faded and his look turned gravely serious. All I could do was nod my head.

"You call me Teacher and Lord, and you are right, for so I am. If I then, your Lord and Teacher, have washed your feet, you also ought to wash one another's feet. For I have given you an example that you also should do just as I have done to you. Truly, truly, I say to you, a servant is not greater than his master, nor is a messenger greater than the one who sent him. If you know these things, blessed are you if you do them. I am not speaking of all of you; I know whom I have chosen. But the Scripture will be fulfilled, 'He who ate my bread has lifted his heel against me.' I am telling you this now, before it takes place, that when it does take place you may believe that I am he. Truly, truly, I say to you, whoever receives the one I send receives me, and whoever receives me receives the one who sent me."

I turned my head and suddenly I was back in the darkened room. A tear started to fall from my cheek as I awoke to the fear I was feeling. *He told me to not lose my joy*, I thought. But I didn't have any joy right then. All I had was an emptiness inside that wanted to be filled. It wanted to be filled with anything. I looked over at my brother who was still holding the basin, almost caressing its hardness. The basin was just as empty as I was. But unlike the vessel, water wouldn't fill my void. I needed something thicker to bridge the aching gap.

"What were you saying about a plan, Peter?" I asked intrepidly.

"Sure you want to hear it?" he asked softly.

Chapter 34

Peter

"Sure you want to hear it?" I asked surprised. I had spent the last hour staring out into the darkness, finding bits of light on which to focus my attention. The flaming torches from far were still flickering, but not as boldly as they were earlier in the night. I didn't know what time of night it was, but I was hoping the sun would be rising soon. I was ready to see some light, but even as I longed for the light, I knew that the planning needed to happen in the dark. I wasn't ready to expose my pain and retaliation in broad daylight. Shame didn't look as shameful in the dark.

"First off, we have to get Judas Iscariot for turning Jesus in," I said bluntly as I sat down in the middle of the room with the others. "If he didn't turn Jesus in, this wouldn't have happened. I don't care what we decide to do to him, but we have to be in agreement, and he has to be punished."

There was silence in the room.

I started to faintly see heads moving and hear a muttering among my brothers, but I couldn't make out what was being said or who was saying it.

"What?" I asked as the commotion started to get louder. "What are you whispering about?"

"You don't know?" Bartholomew asked in shock.

"Don't know what?"

Once again whispers filled the silence.

"Don't know what?" I said a little louder, commanding the room.

Heads once again looked around the room as they all turned and settled on one person.

"Judas is dead," James said depressingly.

"Dead?" I exclaimed with a mixture of anger and resentment that I wasn't there to see him die. "What happened?" I asked, hoping to hear that someone in the group had the nerve to track him down themselves and finish off the backstabber.

No one answered loudly, but instead went back to their incessant murmuring.

"Which one of you did it?" I questioned in the blackness. I waited to hear an enthusiastic roar of applause, but there was none. "Did they do it?" I asked quietly, thinking if they got Jesus, why not get Judas too? Then if they got Judas who turned Jesus in, then they would definitely start coming after the rest of us.

"Who's 'they'?" Matthew asked beside me.

"You know, *they*. The Roman guards. Did the Council command them to attack Judas and kill him?" I asked. "Because if they did, then we need to attack them before they attack us." I immediately jumped up and ran over to the window to scan the city, looking for any sign of life coming this direction. A shadow, a torch, the sound of their leather pteruges slapping against their muscular legs. "They could already be out there."

"Peter, stop it," Mary pleaded. "Just stop it."

"But they could," I started to say before someone broke my chain of thought.

"He killed himself," Matthew said discouragingly.

Chapter 35

Matthew

"He killed himself," I said remorsefully. "After he turned Jesus in, he went out and killed himself."

I waited for Peter to say something hurtful. I didn't know what I would say in response. Did I agree or disagree? My mind was spinning and I didn't have any focal point to slow the whirlpool. On one side I was angry that Judas caused all of this mess and then cowardly killed himself because he couldn't live with the regret. But on the other side, I was saddened for him because the only place he thought he could turn was suicide. I was also relieved he was gone so he couldn't turn the rest of us in. Added to my swirl of emotions, I was sickened with grief because this was my friend whom I loved.

"I just don't understand," I said audibly to the group. "Why did he do all of this?"

"Greed!" Peter exploded. "It was always about the money for him."

Looking back I did see signs of his love of money, but at the time, I thought he was just being a good steward with our means. One example was just a week ago.

We had been in the region of Bethany and just the day before, Jesus had raised Lazarus from the dead. We were having dinner with Lazarus and his two sisters, Martha and Mary. We were reclining around the table talking to Lazarus as if nothing had happened. I had wanted to ask him what he saw while he was dead, but I didn't think it was the right time. There were so many questions, but that wasn't the time to question. It was the time to celebrate.

Mary had come into the room with an expensive ointment made from pure nard and anointed the feet of Jesus. I watched in shock as she started to wipe his feet with her hair. I closed my eyes and the wave of the sweet aroma danced inside me. I knew this was an example of pure devotion. I couldn't remember the last time I did something that seemed so beneath me.

I had been sitting beside Judas Iscariot and he'd leaned over and whispered in my ear, "Why was this ointment not sold for three hundred denarii and given to the poor?"

I'd opened my eyes and shrugged my shoulders to him. It seemed like a good idea, but then Jesus replied. Somehow, Jesus always knew what we whispered or even what we thought. Was it the expression on our face showing what we were thinking?

"Leave her alone, so that she may keep it for the day of my burial. For the poor you always have with you, but you do not always have me," Jesus had said and looked down smiling brightly to Mary. He'd grabbed her smooth fragrant hands and raised her up, hugging her like a dearly loved daughter.

Now we were reclining around the table like we had been a week ago. We had a different Mary in our midst, but most of us were the same.

"Do you think..." I started, but then stopped myself for fear of ridicule.

"Think what?" John asked inquisitively.

"A week ago Jesus raised Lazarus from the dead." I stopped and gazed around the darkened room. "Do you think Jesus is going to rise from the dead?"

I saw a few heads raise a little higher. It was a question that none of them had asked themselves.

I started to have a birth of hope. If Jesus did all of these miracles, including calling the dead Lazarus to come forth out of the tomb, could that be his plan? What if his plan was to die so he could prove himself as the Son of God?

"A dead man can't do anything," Peter said unfazed.

"But what if?" I asked again. But as I said it I saw all the heads that were lifted up a second ago were shaking their heads in remorse.

"If he wanted to prove himself, Matthew," Thomas started kindly, "he would have climbed off of the cross and showed the proof that his wounds had supernaturally healed. Then everyone would have seen the power he had." He let out a heavy breath. "I wish I could believe you, but the truth is, just like Peter said, Jesus is dead."

It was like the seed of hope I just planted was drowned by my tears once again. I didn't want to think about my dashed dreams anymore.

"Maybe he was greedy," I said, wanting to change the subject back to Judas.

"But he gave it back," a fragile voice broke through the darkness.

Chapter 36

Andrew

"But he gave it back," I said timidly. I didn't want anyone to think I was defending Judas, but I also wanted them to know the truth of what I saw.

"Gave what back?" Peter asked confused.

"This morning I went into the city to see what was going on. I was hoping that through the night, Jesus was released because there wasn't anything they could hold him for. As I was walking, I saw Judas running through the streets, bumping into people like a mad man. He never stopped to apologize or see if the people he collided with were all right. This piqued my interest, so I followed him."

"You followed him?" Peter asked deranged. "What were you thinking? If someone saw you, they could have gone after you next!"

"I was thinking…" I stopped and thought about the scornful yet protective words of my older brother. "Actually, I don't know what I was thinking. But if you saw the way he was acting, you would have followed him too."

"So, are you going to tell us what happened?" Peter asked.

I started telling them everything I could remember. My words started coming out, and suddenly it was as if I was there. I was standing at the temple entrance, peeping my head around the corner to see the commotion. The temple was filled with people observing Passover.

Judas came running into the temple pushing past the crowds to find where a few of the chief priests and elders were meeting. I could see him strangling a money bag with his tightly clenched fists. The money inside jingled and clanked with each move he made.

"I have sinned by betraying innocent blood!" he screamed. His facial expressions twitched as he was both crying in regret and shouting in anger. He was like a violent storm, a clashing of two powers.

"What is that to us?" one of the elders smugly asked, looking at the other elders and chief priest who all nodded in agreement.

Judas looked defeated. His tears dried up. His anger froze. It was as if he was seeing the truth for the first time. That these men whom he had turned to were now turning their backs on him. He saw the double standard written on each of their faces. He had turned his back on Jesus as well.

"See to it yourself," the elder said, shrugging his shoulders nonchalantly then immediately going back to their conversation. They ignored Judas as if he wasn't even standing there. Trembling. Flinching. Almost convulsing.

"Here's your money back," he said as he loosened the money bag and flipped it over. He didn't watch the trickling pieces of silver fall and jump around on the ground. He kept his head up and watched the chief priest. "I'm not going to need it anymore."

He turned and slowly walked out of the temple. I was startled by the sudden flip of persona. He went in as a crazed man that seemed possessed and left as a hollowed shell. I didn't hide as he walked past me, and he didn't even notice my presence.

I thought about saying something to him, but I didn't know what to say. I had seen it all first hand.

He walked the dusty roads to a small area outside of the town and stood under a tree for some time. I watched from the distance. The area was peaceful. The sky was blue. The sun was shining. The white fluffy clouds overhead danced through the sky like new-found lovers. I turned my back to him when I heard the shouts and screams from the city, and my heart sank.

"Crucify!" I could clearly hear them saying, but then I heard a name. A name I didn't want to hear. "Whom do you want me to release for you: Barabbas, or Jesus who is called Christ?" the question echoed through the city up to the lonely hill where Judas and I were standing.

They chanted his name like he was a god and not a murderer. They screamed his name as if he was innocent. They yelled, "Barabbas!"

My heart sank at the sound of his name. I stood amazed looking down over the city and knew I needed to get to safety as soon as possible. That's when another sound startled me from behind.

The crack of a branch.

I turned around and saw Judas lying under the tree with a noose around his neck and a broken limb laying over his dead body. Blood was seeping through his robe in his midsection.

One minute he was standing there, and the next, he was dead.

"Oh, Andrew," Mary moaned as I finished my story. She got up from her seat beside John and rushed over to me. "I'm so sorry you had to see that."

"I'm glad I saw it," I said solemnly. "Because there is no telling what people would be saying about him if I didn't."

"They would make something up," Matthew agreed. "They always do."

We sat in silence to allow John, Peter, and Mary time to let the words sink in. We all understood how, in a split second, life could be turned to death. I mulled over my thoughts and circled back to Peter.

"So, what is your next step in your plan since Judas is already gone?" I asked distantly. I didn't want to spend the rest of the night sulking over Judas.

"Next is the guards," Peter answer defiantly. "Definitely the guards."

Chapter 37

Peter

"Next is the guards," I answered confidently. "Definitely the guards."

There was a hush in the circle. Everyone was attentive to my next words. Not everyone was going to agree, but right now, everyone wanted to hear.

"We have all day tomorrow to figure out how it needs to be done, but my suggestion is to surprise attack them when they are alone. Then, one by one, we can weaken their defense," I said strategically.

"One by one?" Thaddaeus asked skeptically. "That's going to take forever to get revenge on what they have done." The rest of the group started to agree with Thaddaeus, silently nodding their heads.

"But think about it," I said looking around the circle, catching a few gazes since my eyes had finally somewhat adjusted to the darkness. "If we get a few of them ourselves, then maybe others will start following us." I stopped and started to imagine the possibilities. We had been under Roman law and persecution for too long. "It's time to rise up and get our freedom back. I know there are other people out there," I said pointing out the window, "who feel caged like we do right now."

I wanted to let that sink in. I knew they had heard all their lives that they wanted the stronghold of the Roman government off of their shoulders. I knew I wasn't saying anything new. I knew they were probably thinking similar things three years ago.

"Peter, I think you are right that they want their freedom. But I don't think they are going to want to follow us," Thaddaeus commented again. "They are going to see us as the group who followed the man they just killed. Everyone in the city is going to know we were his followers. If they don't, our friends and families will tell them we are just a bunch of young men rebelling."

"I know that's what people will think about me," John feebly said. "I've been told my whole life that I'm just a kid."

"You may have been a kid yesterday," I said with a booming tone. "But you're a man today."

"So, murdering someone makes you a man?" John questioned with an undertone of disgust. "What would Jesus say about this?"

"Jesus is gone, John!" Peter snapped. "Jesus is dead and he's not coming back."

"I think what John is trying to say, Peter…" Mary started before she was quickly hushed.

"I think this discussion is best left for just the men," I interrupted.

I saw Mary slowly rise from her position beside Andrew. "I think that's my sign to leave."

"Mary, stop," I said, not ashamed of what I said, but fearful of where she was going. "You can't go out this time of night. Something may happen to you."

"I think I am safer out there," she said sorrowfully, "than in here."

Chapter 38

Mary Magdalene

"I think I am safer out there, than in here," I painfully said. I didn't want to give Peter the satisfaction of hearing my voice quiver, but I was shaking on the inside. I was shaking from the evil being plotted. I was on edge from the callousness of their schemes. I was shattered from their sexist remark. Jesus had never looked at me like I was less than a man. He always saw me as an equal. I had never felt that equality was something I could gain, but it seemed like I was losing my foothold.

All my life I had heard the expression, son of Abraham. That phrase was said to good Jewish boys who adhered to their fathers or rabbis, but never had I heard anyone say something like that to a woman. That was until Jesus.

Jesus had been teaching in the synagogue on the Sabbath when he saw a woman beaten down with physical pain and emotional scorn from the world. "Woman, you are freed from your disability." He'd touched her and she'd immediately straightened. She had been walking with back issues for eighteen years, not ever able to look anyone in their eyes because her back didn't allow it and she didn't want to face the ridicule.

Instead of praising Jesus, some of the people had rebuked him. "There are six days in which work ought to be done. Come on those days and be healed, and not on the Sabbath day."

I was utterly speechless. Jesus had just healed a woman, removing her affliction and they were scolding him for which day of the week he showed kindness.

"You hypocrites!" Jesus commanded. "Does not each of you on the Sabbath untie his ox or his donkey from the manger and lead it away to water? And ought not this woman, a daughter of Abraham whom Satan bound for eighteen years, be loosed from this bond on the Sabbath day?"

He had once again silenced his oppressors. They lowered their heads in shame and disgrace, but the healed woman raised hers with a radiant smile. I would never forget that. It wasn't just the miracle I would always cherish, but the words he spoke. He didn't just speak them in his rebuttal, but he spoke them again.

"Daughter of Abraham, what is your name?" he'd asked as he smiled at the beautiful woman.

I didn't recall what she said her name was, but to me, her name and my name and all the women before and after me would be called daughter of Abraham. From that moment I knew that my sex wasn't going to limit or define my future. I was a daughter of God. I wasn't just a woman. I was His daughter that He loved dearly.

I started walking down the steps when I heard a pair of footsteps running behind me.

"Mary, I'm going with you," John said.

I always loved John. I mean, I loved all the men in that room, even Peter because I knew in his heart he didn't mean what he just said. But it still hurt. But John was too precious to not love differently.

He had a caring heart and was free with his emotions. He showed it this afternoon when he stayed with me while Jesus was dying.

"John, you need to stay here," I whispered.

"It's not safe out here," he said puffing his chest out a little more.

I was flattered. Little John was trying to be the protector when most of the time he was the one needing protection. That is what I loved about him – his genuineness to rise to any occasion at a moment's notice.

"John, listen to me," I said calmly. "You need to stay here and listen to what they are plotting. Peter is upset, and good things don't come out of people when they are angry. You need to be the voice of reason. I need you to stay here and listen," I said leaning over and kissing him on the cheek. "I love you, John. You are just as Jesus always said you were."

"But…" he started to say until I placed my finger to his lips and shook my head.

"Go back up there for the both of us, John. I will see you tomorrow."

I knew he didn't want to go and I felt encouraged about that. But I knew it was for the best interest of everyone for him to stay.

The walk back to Mary's wasn't too far. I only needed Peter and John earlier because I didn't know where the other men were hiding.

I covered my head with my veil and left the home. I started walking the lonely streets under the cloudy sky. Occasionally the moon peeked through the cloud, but each parting wasn't for long. The rain continued to sprinkle on top of my head as I walked the alleyways. I had been gone for about ten minutes and had only a few more turns before I was back at Mary's. Silence was all I heard. Everyone was asleep.

Until I heard a faint splash behind me. I thought it was probably nothing, my naivety hoping for safety. Then I heard another splash.

Then another.

And another until the splashes were drowned out by the running of a pair of feet behind me. I turned my head to see who was coming, and he was right behind me.

"Well, why are you out here all alone, pretty lady?" he said coarsely. "It's not safe," he said as he grabbed me from behind. I tried to scream, but he had already covered my mouth.

The clouds parted and I saw a glimpse of his face. Fear surged. Panic struck. Knots choked my stomach as he started to choke my neck. I had seen him before.

"Be good or I won't," he cooed menacingly.

Chapter 39
Barabbas

"Be good or I won't," I said, almost chuckling to myself as I saw my newest victim. I wanted to say a prayer of thanks as the moon parted showing me the exquisite beauty I would have tonight. The look in her eyes made me even more aroused.

I kept one hand sealed over her mouth and the other tightly locked around her throat. If she tried anything, I could break her scrawny neck with one twist and she knew it. She'd heard the stories about me. She'd heard the tales in the marketplace or from her friends warning of the deeds I had done. Sadly, it wasn't all true. I heard them tell me once of the crimes they thought I had committed: robbery, murder, insurrection. I would shake my head and tell them they were wrong.

Technically, I wasn't lying. They were wrong.

I had done many more things than what they told me. I was often amused at how the truth and the lie sometimes went hand in hand.

People might ask how I could murder someone without any remorse.

But I didn't see it as murder. I just saw myself as a man getting vengeance for the wrongs done to me. That's not murder. That's self-defense.

That's how I lived without any inner demons haunting me. I didn't let my dark side scare me. I played with it.

I pushed her against the wall and banged her head against it twice. I watched as her eyes squinted in pain.

A torrid thought pranced through my devilish mind: *I wonder if she was one of the people who requested my release today?*

Yesterday I was brought in front of Pilate and the crowd and he asked them who they wanted released. I could still hear them. It was music to my ears. Some might think my freedom would have changed me, but it just caused the fire to grow stronger. I got away with my crimes again, and I was eager to see how many more times I could get away with it.

"Away with this man, and release to us Barabbas," someone had screamed before the rest of the crowd joined in.

"Why do you want to release a murderer back onto the streets? What if I release Jesus instead?" Pilate rephrased, but they didn't want to hear it.

"We want Barabbas! We want Barabbas! Barabbas! Barabbas!" the crowd had roared, getting louder and louder each time. It was a heavenly sound, if I believed in heaven. Which I didn't.

They released me and I watched from afar as the three men died. One man suffered in my place, an innocent man at that, so I was told. One might think I would feel remorse, but all I did was laugh at his expense.

"Did you say my name today?" I whispered into the maiden's ear, pressing my body into hers. "I want to hear you say my name again tonight," I whispered with sexually starved breath. "I want my name to be the last thing you say."

A tear started to run down her cheek, trickling over my fingers. I couldn't help myself. I leaned closer to her face and licked the teardrop dangling on my knuckle.

"Tastes sweet," I moaned. "Sweet as honey. Come on, let me taste more of your sugary tears."

Her eyes darted toward the alley's opening. My eyes followed where she was looking. I heard two men's voices and the splashing of water with each of their steps.

"If you make one sound, I will…" I started to stay, but it was too late. She kneed me.

I let go of my grip and fell to the ground.

"Help!" she screamed as I tried to crawl into the shadows.

She ran to the alley's entrance and started shouting and pointing in my direction.

"Where is he?"

Chapter 40
Longinus

"Where is he?" I asked, as my comrade Classius and I immediately started hurrying down the darkened alley. We waived our torches and I could see a pair of legs hiding behind a large cistern.

Classius gave me his torch and then reached down, pulling up the wounded man. His face was just as menacing as it had been earlier in the day, but now he was flinching in pain. "So, Barabbas," he said, pressing his back onto the wall. "You couldn't make it a day without trying to rape someone."

"I wasn't just going to rape her," he laughed as he spit into Classius' face. "She's just as useless as an old ox," he hissed. "Just let me go and I promise I won't do it again."

"Sure," I nodded. "That's honest."

"Well," Barabbas chuckled like he was talking to long-time friends, "it was worth a try."

"What should we do with him?" Classius asked, looking at Barabbas and then me.

"Lock him up, I guess," I said pulling out a pair of shackles from the sack on my belt. "You don't deserve to be given another chance."

"They'll let me go," Barabbas snorted. "They always do and then I'll be out on the streets again."

A look of rage went over Classius with those words. "You know, you are right." He pulled out his sword and drove it into Barabbas' chest.

The criminal's knees buckled as Classius' sword remained in his chest.

"Classius!" I barked, looking around to see if anyone saw what just happened.

"You heard him, he was just going to keep doing it. Do you want him to come after your wife?" Classius asked matter-of-factly as he pulled out his sword and wiped it clean on the dead man's robe. "He deserved to die this afternoon."

"But it wasn't your call," I said, standing my ground.

"Go home and ask your wife if she feels safer knowing there is one less rapist and murderer off the streets tonight," Classius said as he kicked the body to the wall to be hidden until morning.

I didn't disagree with him. He had a point. However, it wasn't our job to be the judge. It was our job to deliver the sentence.

"The way I see it, we did our job tonight," he smiled. "Another execution. There just wasn't a crowd to see it."

"What about the body?" I asked, knowing we just couldn't leave a dead man in the alley.

"Just leave it," he said casually as he started to walk away. "Whoever finds him will think he got what he deserved. They will think it was an act of vengeance for some of his past crimes."

"It just doesn't seem right," I muttered to myself.

"I thought you were just saying the man who died today didn't deserve to die," Classius replied. "So, this is us correcting that error. All is well in the world now."

"I'm not sure about that," I mumbled to myself as I left the corpse.

I left the alley and found the woman we just saved, shaking and crying. Classius walked right past her, didn't even acknowledge her, but I couldn't ignore her and leave.

"It's okay; he's not going to hurt you again," I stated coolly, bending down to look the woman in her eyes. I raised my torch so she could see a friendly face in this dark night. Usually the Roman guards did not have a good relationship with the citizens, but I wanted her to know I was one of the good ones.

"You coming?" Classius asked up the road.

"I'll see you tomorrow," I said as Classius walked away.

She looked into my eyes and they locked. She tilted her head as if trying to remember where she had seen me and suddenly the thought came into my mind as well. I gazed onto her features, looking intently at the brightness in her eyes, the curvature of her nose, the slanting of her cheekbones. I did all I could to remember how I knew her.

"You look familiar," I finally said.

"You too," she nodded in agreement.

I helped her to her feet and asked where she was going. She said it wasn't far. I offered to walk her home and she kindly accepted the invitation. I think the last ten minutes had upset her as it would have anyone in her situation.

We were both silent as we walked. I held the torch high, so she could see her surroundings, but as we were walking, it seemed like she was looking at me more than the road. We twisted and turned through the roads until she stopped in front of a small home.

"Thank you for walking me home," she kindly said as she smiled appreciatively.

135

"Stay safe," I smiled back. "My name is Longinus by the way."

"Pleased to meet you, Longinus. My name is Mary," she said bowing her head in honor to a Roman guard. "And if you ever need anything, just let me know."

As she walked into the home, I saw various people in the room sleeping, but the woman at the table was muttering something to herself.

"My soul magnifies the Lord," she said as I walked away, heading home to check on my lovely wife. I knew Classius was correct. My wife was going to be relieved Barabbas wasn't around anymore.

Chapter 41
Mary

"My soul magnifies the Lord," I prayed as I had a hundred times before, but tonight – tonight it felt different. I stopped and hoped I could continue the prayer with reverence. But right now, scorn and pain were seeping through the precious words, tainting them with bitterness and desolation.

But I knew I couldn't stop. I couldn't. I started once again and my mind went back to the moment when I first said these words.

"And my spirit rejoices in God my Savior," I wept, recalling the memories of when I was with child staying with my aunt and uncle in a small town in Judah. They'd never once looked at me with contempt, because the instant I walked into their home, Elizabeth had embraced me with love and devotion. She'd taken off the veil I wore to hide my shame from the words people had said to my face. She looked me in my eyes and smiled. I remembered crumbling into her arms. My parents had wanted me to leave so I wouldn't have to face the ridicule anymore. I was expecting to live in seclusion. But Elizabeth unbound me.

"Blessed are you among women, and blessed is the fruit of your womb!" my aunt had exclaimed with joyful exuberance. She had started to dance as her husband, Zechariah, silently joined in the rejoicing. I hadn't felt this loved in some time. I hadn't felt this worthy, even though I knew I was in a situation not from my own doing. But I had been chosen. To hear Elizabeth say those words, it was the confirmation I needed to assure myself I wasn't crazy. An angel really had come to me.

"For he has looked on this humble estate of his servant." As I said these words, I wondered, *Is he looking upon my humble state now?* I let that question sit and churn in my mind. I didn't know if I felt comforted or contempt knowing He was looking upon me now. *If you see me, why did you do this, God?*

"For behold, from now on all generations will call me blessed," I started to sob. I regaled in the happy moment when I first uttered this phrase, recalling the loving touch Elizabeth gave to me. I went from feeling abused and tormented in Nazareth to feeling blessed with my aunt and uncle. It only took one kind word to help erase the tarnished words that were thrown like rocks at my feet. But I didn't feel blessed anymore.

"For He who is mighty has done great things for me, and holy is His name." I tried my best to say these words with praise, but as the words came forth it was less like praise and more like spit. I wanted with all my heart to say these words with their intended meaning, but I just couldn't. I couldn't see that He had done a great thing for me today.

"And His mercy is for those who fear him from generation to generation." *What mercy?* I selfishly thought as tears streamed down my cheek. What mercy, indeed? I had so much fear in my bones, but I didn't feel His mercy. No, I didn't feel any type of comfort.

"He has shown strength with his arm; he has scattered the proud in the thoughts of their hearts." I started to heave at the thought of my son being mocked by the proud men I used to revere. The proud, ambitious driven council stopped at nothing to kill my beloved son – but they weren't scattered. I was.

"He has brought down the mighty from their thrones and exalted those of humble estate; he has filled the hungry with good things, and the rich he has sent away empty." I clenched my hands, forming balls of fists. I had done the best I could, raising a family after the death of my husband, Joseph. Jesus did the best he could, picking up the carpentry skills Joseph had taught him. I knew I needed to feel blessed for not ever being in need, but the rich were not empty. The rich were celebrating tonight, I thought as I opened my eyes and uncurled my hands. They celebrated as I sat there with empty hands. I had never felt this low before. Never. I never sat on a throne, and I definitely never would.

I stared off into the distance. I didn't know what I was looking at. It was as if I was in a trance, one that beckoned me to finish this song I had sung for years. But tonight I wasn't singing. There was no reason to sing.

"He has helped his servant Israel, in remembrance of his mercy, as he spoke to our fathers, to Abraham and to his offspring forever. Where is my help, my Lord? Where is my, help?" I stammered out, pounding my fist onto the wooden table Joseph had carved. It had been a present for one of our anniversaries. "Where is my help, Lord? I need it now!" I stopped and laid my head on the table, feeling the scratches born through years of dinners and festivities – times of celebrations with thankfulness and hope. I traced my finger along the wood and kept moaning, "Where is my help, my Lord? Where is it?"

"I'll help you."

Chapter 42

Mary Magdalene

"I'll help you," I said as Mary looked up, eyes swollen from the many tears she had cried tonight.

"I know," she said as she stood up to greet me with a hug. "I know, dear."

I didn't know what it was, but as she hugged me all my strength fell away. I was like a glass orb colliding with the hard ground, breaking into millions of glass shards – each one too small to see with the naked eye.

I was breaking from the memory of being held against my will only minutes earlier as Barabbas spoke death into my ears like it was nothing. But now, I was being held with love as she whispered words of life.

I was crumbling with the realization that Peter saw me as nothing more than a woman he could command. But now, I was being spoken to with affirmation and respect.

I was falling apart with the notion that the last three years of Jesus' words of love and forgiveness were being washed away with the tides from the Sea of Vengeance. But now, I was being comforted with the love I so dearly wanted to see through the night.

I was eroding with the realization that the world I knew last week was gone. Her embrace couldn't erase the memory of events from earlier this week.

Jesus had been welcomed into Jerusalem with open arms by a large crowd who had been following him, listening to his teachings.

When they heard he was coming, they immediately took their palm branches to greet him.

"Hosanna!" they had yelled in honor as Jesus came by riding a donkey's colt. "Blessed is he who comes in the name of the Lord, even the King of Israel!"

I had stood amazed among the crowd. I couldn't believe my eyes and ears with the reception he was getting. But my heart had been enthralled, as though it was going to explode with the excitement in the air. I had always loved Passover with all of its symbolism and promise – God would always provide. But this Passover I knew was going to be different. This one was going to be one I would never forget.

As a young girl, I had hated the idea of my father sacrificing a precious lamb. He would bring the lamb home, but I could never look at it because I knew if I looked I would feel shame for the lamb having to shed its blood for my sins.

"Mary," he would say in a tender voice, "look at the lamb."

But I couldn't. I would just shake my head with my eyes closed. I couldn't look at the innocent creature making the baaing sounds that would make me laugh on any other occasion. But during the week of Passover, the baaing didn't make me smile. It made me tear up.

Jesus had waved to the people, touching those approaching him and speaking words of love and hope, just as he did every other day of his life. This wasn't a political move or an act. I had seen him live what he taught. He was genuine.

As Jesus had come into town, I knew my father was on the other side of the city getting the lamb for the family as they were being herded into the city for their preparations. As Jesus came by on the donkey, he'd looked into my eyes and I distinctly heard my father's voice as if he was standing next to me.

"Mary, look at the lamb."

I didn't know then why my father's voice and memory surfaced during Jesus' triumphal entry. But I knew now.

As Jesus was hanging on the cross, I kept hearing my father's voice. I didn't want to listen, but it kept repeating the haunting words of my childhood until it became deafening. I just wanted the words to stop. I wanted everything to stop.

"Mary, look at the lamb, dear. Please Mary, the lamb is dying for you," my father said softly one last time.

I looked up.

"Just let it out, dear," Mary said as she continued to rock me in her arms. "Just let it out." As I cried on her shoulder I noticed she wasn't crying. That was a sign of a true mother, to muster up strength for moments like this.

We rocked each other in our arms until we couldn't rock anymore and fell asleep.

THE NEXT DAY

Chapter 43

Caiaphas – Jewish Priest

I always hated going to the Roman government for assistance. It felt beneath me to ask for help, especially, since they were Romans. A few other priests met late last night and decided we needed to swallow our pride and request additional resources over the next few days. We had hoped that the Jesus situation would be resolved by his death, but like many revolutionaries in the past, their ragtag team of misfits usually caused a few more spills before the total mess was cleaned up. We were just taking some precautionary measures.

We entered the palace courts and none of the guards bowed in honor of me. *I hated the Romans.*

"Good day, Pilate," I greeted warmly as the three other priests with me kindly added their salutations.

"Caiaphas, did you sleep well last night?" Pilate cunningly asked.

I knew what he was implying. He had made a theatrical production of his sentence yesterday.

"I am innocent of this man's blood; see to it yourself," Pilate had said as he'd taken water and washed his hands before the screaming crowd. He'd looked over at me and shaken his head unapologetically. "If Barabbas is who you want released, Barabbas is who you will get!"

"Barabbas!" the crowd had roared.

Many would have thought I would be pleased with how the plan was falling into place, but his spectacle was making me look like a whining child. I detested the high and mighty way the Romans always looked at me.

"I did indeed," I lied. I had actually tossed and turned all night wondering what the rest of Jesus' followers were planning to do. He probably knew I didn't sleep well since I was in his palace court at the break of dawn.

"Any regrets from yesterday?" Pilate asked calmly as he paced around the court.

"Regrets?" I asked astonished, looking at my fellow priests for affirmation. "Why would we have any regrets?"

"I don't know," Pilate said shrugging his shoulders nonchalantly. "Most people do."

"Well, I'm not like most people," I said forcefully.

"You are correct there," Pilate said with a cunning grin and a cockeyed look.

I hated the Romans.

I wanted to get back to the point of why we were there this morning. "Sir," I started, biting my tongue in disgust at the reverent word, "we remember how that impostor said while he was still alive, 'After three days I will rise.' Therefore, order the tomb to be made secure until the third day, lest his disciples go and steal him away and tell the people, 'He has risen from the dead,' and the last fraud will be worse than the first."

"I heard the curtain in your temple was torn yesterday," Pilate inquired, changing the subject.

Did he not hear me? I wondered. *Or was he just playing me?* "Yes, yes the *veil* was torn, sir," I answered, wanting to get back to my request. "Back to our concern," I started, but I was interrupted again.

"How did the veil split, right down the middle?' Pilate asked inquisitively. "From what I have been told that veil is very thick and not easy to cut."

I didn't want to discuss the veil. That was not the purpose of this visit. I didn't want to speak to him on Jewish rituals and beliefs, just so he could turn his nose to our heritage.

"I asked you a question, Caiaphas," Pilate said, stopping his casual stroll to look directly into my eyes. "How did the veil split?"

"The earthquake must have torn the veil," I said agitatedly. "It is being repaired as we speak."

"That is a pity, especially with your Passover celebration." Pilate clicked his tongue in sympathy. "I know that veil is highly revered by you. If there is anything I can do to help you, please let me know."

"You can guard the tomb!" I snapped back angrily. Taking a deep breath, I controlled my tone. "You can have your soldiers guard the tomb, sir."

Pilate started to walk again. "Very well. You have a guard of soldiers. Go, make it as secure as you can," he said waving us away and turning to a Roman guard. "Go get Maximus and the guards."

"Thank you, Pilate," I said appreciatively, even though it was forced. We turned to leave and I wanted to leave dignified.

"Oh, Caiaphas," Pilate said from across the court.

"Yes, Pilate," I said turning his way.

"Get some rest today, Caiaphas," he said smugly. "My men will take care of your rebellion."

I was about to mutter something I had wanted to say for years, but my friends quickly stood in front of me and gave their thanks.

146

Chapter 44

Pilate – Governor of Judea

"My men will take care of your rebellion," I said watching the priest stammer in aggravation as they quickly stomped away.

I should hate to find enjoyment out of ridiculing them, but I don't. It's just one of the many perks of being governor. I needed to find something to smile about after my wife was upset I didn't do more to save Jesus yesterday before the crowd.

"Whom do you want me to release for you: Barabbas, or Jesus who is called Christ?" I had announced before the crowd. I was expecting everyone to say Jesus, especially after hearing how he was adorned like royalty earlier in the week.

As I asked the question, my wife leaned over and pleaded with me. "Have nothing to do with this righteous man, for I have suffered much because of him today in a dream."

"It's going to be okay," I assured her. "The crowd will surely not want Barabbas to be released," I grinned. "Jesus hasn't done anything against them, but Barabbas is a cruel man."

I sat on my judgment seat and asked once again, "Which of these two do you want me to release to you?"

My ears burned at the name they wanted to release.

I turned to look at my wife who lowered her head and shook it in disbelief. "You have to stop it," she muttered softly. She lifted her head and looked me in the eyes. "You must. You have to stop this, Pilate."

My wife hardly ever interfered in my position, but when she said something, I always tried my best to listen. I nodded to her and started again.

"Why?" I asked, pleading to the crowd. "What evil has he done?"

But the crowd had continued to scream madly. "Let him be crucified! We want Barabbas!"

I looked over at my wife who quickly turned her gaze away from me. I had done many things in our marriage she didn't approve of, but she always wore the title as governor's wife with pride.

"I tried," I said, stretching my hand to hers, but she quickly got up from her seat and walked away.

I can't be certain of what she said, but I believe it wasn't good from the looks the guards gave me as she passed by them.

The crowd continued to roar, louder and louder each time.

"Barabbas!"

"Barabbas!"

"Barabbas!"

"Maximus!" one of the guards announced, bringing me back to the present as an older soldier came marching into the palace courts followed by a band of warriors that looked menacing and equipped for battle.

"You called for me, sir," Maximus said as he bowed.

"Yes," I stated, shaking off the memory and admiring the fine quality of the soldiers in our province. They were strong, capable, and ready. "You were correct with your assumption. The Jewish priests want some soldiers to guard the tomb."

"I just wanted to warn you about what I was hearing around the city last night, sir," he said, not taking any credit for his forthcoming.

"So, do you have some guards for this duty?" I asked. "It shouldn't be a hard task and shouldn't be for very long. They just want a guard at the tomb for a few days."

"Yes, Pilate," he announced and then started calling out names as each soldier stood to attention and barked, "Yes, sir."

I watched as a group of half a dozen men stepped forward.

"Longinus!" Maximus shouted as a strapping man stepped away from the line of soldiers.

"Yes, sir!"

Chapter 45

Longinus

"Yes, sir!" I announced before Pilate and Maximus. I was relieved he had listened to my request to stand guard before the tomb. I had already decided if my name wasn't called, I would switch duties with anyone who was assigned. I still didn't know why I had this compelling feeling, but something was still unsettled in my core.

It had been a long day yesterday and by the time I got home, my wife had been asleep for hours. This morning she had woken up before me, fixed me something to eat, and greeted me with a nice kiss and a plate of her best cooking.

"How are you doing this morning?" she'd asked as she sat down at the table with me.

"Tired," I'd replied with my eyes still drooping as the sun slowly rose in the distance.

"They are working you too much," she'd stated, but she knew I couldn't say anything. I was just a soldier who did as he was commanded. "You didn't get in until late last night."

"I know. We had a lot to get finished," I'd said taking a bite of the bread she had made the day before.

"I'm scared," she had said with a quivering voice.

"Why, Helena?" I'd asked, laying down my bread and scooping her face into my thick, strong hands. "I'm not going to let anything happen to you."

She'd nodded as a few tears fell. I brushed each one away with my thumb.

"You have nothing to be afraid of. I'm right here."

She had wiped her eyes and her nose, stood up, and walked over to the window. "It's stupid. Why did they have to let that murderer go yesterday?"

"I don't know. That was stupid."

"Now, there is a murderer out there," she'd huffed in fear as she walked away from the window. "All I thought about last night when you weren't here was, could he get me? When I go to the market should I be afraid? I mean, I'm a Roman citizen, and he's someone who would come after me just because I'm not from around here."

I had stood and embraced my trembling wife. I breathed in and out, allowing her to feel my lungs fill with air, hoping that my deep breaths would cause her to take a few of her own. She'd looked up at me and smiled. "I always feel safe in your arms."

"My arms are always here for you," I had said kissing her again.

"Except for when you're not here."

"He's not going to get you," I had said, wondering how much I should tell.

"How do you know?" I couldn't blame her for doubting me.

"I just know." I had winked at her playfully, but she wasn't in a mocking mood. Her fear was real. "Let's just say I know for sure he's not going to be harming anyone, ever again."

She'd looked into my eyes and I thought she understood.

"You?" she had asked in shock.

I had shaken my head. "It wasn't me."

"Classius?" she'd asked, starting to go down her mental list of the men in my unit.

151

"It doesn't matter who, but you can rest assured you are safe."

She'd stretched her neck and kissed me one more time before sitting back down at the table, holding my hand. We were a team and she was a member I would die for.

"You hear things around the town," I had said as I tore off a piece of the bread.

She'd nodded as she grabbed a piece from my plate and tossed it into her mouth before I could stop her. Her grin made my life worth living.

"What do you know about Jesus who died yesterday?"

"Some say he was a nice man. Others say he was a healer. A few said he was a liar." She'd shrugged her shoulders.

"Who do *you* think he was?"

"I don't know." She had laughed as she stood up to get me another piece of fruit to eat.

"No, really. Who do you think he was?"

She'd come back to the table with a few figs. "A man who got a bad deal."

"Do you think he was anything special?" I'd asked, leaving the figs untouched.

"Special?" She'd thought for a second. "You're the only one special to me," she said. "Is something on your mind?"

"Something just didn't feel right yesterday," I'd said honestly. I had hid many things from Helena. She didn't need to know everything I had to do each day in my line of work. I didn't want her eyes to look at me with shame or embarrassment. I wanted her to look at me like the man she thought I was.

"I think it was the change in the weather," she'd said.

"Maybe that was it," I had muttered eating a few more nuts. "Maybe it was the weather."

Now that I had my orders to stand guard this evening, I decided to go back home and get some rest before my midnight shift started.

I walked through the city streets and felt a change in the air. I couldn't put my finger on it, but it definitely wasn't the weather. It was something else.

"Please madam, please," I heard a man with dark skin plead as I walked by a home. "I have money."

Chapter 46

Simon of Cyrene

"Please madam, please. I have money. I just want to buy some food for my family," I begged at the door. Everything was closed for the Sabbath and I didn't plan for the events of yesterday.

"Why should I give you some of my food?" the woman protested, standing in the opening so I couldn't break in.

"I don't want you to give it to me for free," I said pulling out my money. "I have money and everything is closed. I just want to feed my family."

"How do you have money?" she asked degradingly.

I lowered my head and walked away. I knew I wouldn't be getting anything from her. Whenever people looked at me, they always assumed I was a slave. But just because my skin was darker didn't mean I was a slave. I was a free man with a wife and children to protect.

I turned down a road and remembered I had been on this road the day before. It seemed bigger than yesterday, but the crowds along the sides had made it feel more confined. I smiled at people as I passed, but none of them smiled back. I didn't know for sure if it was because of where I was from or if they remembered me from yesterday.

There had been a man carrying a bloody wooden beam down this road, falling and tumbling from the torture he endured and the weight of the heavy log along his back. He had fallen right in front of where my wife, my two sons, and I were standing. I had reached over to cover my kids' eyes from the gruesome sight. I was wondering why I

154

brought them into the city that day. They didn't need to see this. We had come in to just get a few things for our meal and somehow ended up on the route to Golgotha.

"You!" a guard had shouted.

I had looked around wondering who he was speaking to, but then he'd shouted again.

"I'm talking to you!"

I quickly gave him my attention and asked, "Me?"

"Yes, are you deaf?" he'd croaked as the crowd roared in laughter. "Carry it!"

I had stood dumbfounded. "I can't leave my family," I pleaded as my wife clutched onto my hand, begging me not to leave them.

"They will be right here when you get done, now pick it up!" the guard commanded, spitting into my face.

I had quickly jumped into the street and helped the broken and bleeding man. I'd tossed the wooden beam to his side as his arms were trembling from exhaustion. As I lifted up the wood, pieces of skin ripped off of his body and blood sprinkled the dusty road. I'd looked past the wounds and into his eyes as he turned his head.

I reached down to help him back to his feet.

His feet had been wobbly, as rivers of blood ran down his thighs and calves. Every step he took left a bloody footprint behind.

"I'm sorry, Simon," he'd muttered as his arms hung around my neck. "I'm so sorry."

How did he know my name?

Suddenly, I had felt a strength in my being that rejuvenated my body and spirit. A stronghold gave me the determination to carry this man's cross with dignity. He started hobbling ahead of me and I'd gladly carried the weight the rest of the way to the place of the skull with my head held high. I wasn't ashamed of who I was. The guard may have chosen me because of how I looked, but I wasn't going to let that define me. With every step he took, I was there to help him. I felt like he would have done the same thing for me if our roles had been reversed.

It was the first time someone of his stature had called me by my name. He didn't even know me. We had never met. But yet, even as he was in agony he still looked past my outward appearance and called me by my name.

When we had come to the place where his cross was going to be mounted, I didn't know what to do. I didn't want to leave him. Even though we had never met, I felt a connection with him I had never felt before.

"Thank you, Simon," he'd said with a gasping breath. "You are not what they say you are, no matter the lifetime of crosses you have carried. You are the son of the most high God. Always remember that. You are His."

I had looked down at the man who was hours away from death, and instead of me consoling him, he was consoling me for a lifetime of snide remarks, prejudicial slurs, and degrading comments. He'd looked into my eyes one last time and then rolled onto the cross where he was nailed through the feet and wrists.

I am the son of the most high God, I thought now, proudly walking through the remainder of the street with my head held high. I am a free man. The labels people gave me were not the labels I wore. I was who he said I was.

"Excuse me," I said as I approached a man a few streets away from where I first carried the cross, "but can I buy some food from you?"

"Keep your money," he said as he walked inside and came back with an arm full of goods. "Here you go."

Chapter 47

John

"Keep your money," I said and walked back up the stairs and started grabbing a few things from the table.

"Where are you going with those?" Peter asked, waking up from a few hours of rest.

"Someone asked if I could give him some food," I said turning to head back down the stairs.

"You can't give him our food, John," he snapped, jumping up from the floor and running down the stairs. "We need that for us."

"We can get more food," I answered bewildered. "He needs it."

"John, you're not thinking," Peter said jamming his finger onto my head. "We don't know how long we are going to be hiding and we need to keep these goods for us."

I ignored him and made my way out the passageway to the street and handed the man the food. "Here you go."

"Thank you, son. Thank you!" he beamed as he walked away looking at the food in his arms in amazement.

"You can't go about giving away our food, John! That was ours!" Peter shouted disgruntled, stomping back up the stairs in rage.

"We will find more food." I followed him and everyone started to move around on the floor from the booming sounds of Peter's voice and steps. "We will. We've gotten food in more dire situations before."

I remembered when Jesus was teaching one day in Bethsaida and a large crowd had gathered; well over five thousand people had come to listen to his words. I remembered looking at the crowd, amazed at how

Jesus could speak and people of all kinds could understand everything he was saying. He never spoke above or below them. He somehow always spoke to everyone's level.

"Send the crowd away to go into the surrounding villages and countryside to find lodging and get provisions, for we are here in a desolate place," one of my brothers had said, but Jesus amazed us all.

"You give them something to eat," he'd said rationally. But as I had looked at the crowd it sounded ludicrous.

"How?" I'd asked Jesus, but he just shook his head.

Someone came up and said, "We have no more than five loaves and two fish – unless we are to go and buy food for all these people."

"Have them sit down in groups of about fifty each," Jesus had said as he took the measly portions.

I walked around the hillside and asked people to congregate and form circles. They'd thought I was strange, and I didn't blame their weird looks because I thought it was strange as well. I recalled saying, "I don't know, Jesus said to just do it," when one person asked why they had to move.

Jesus had given each of us a basket with some food in it and said to pass it around. I looked in the basket and thought, *This wouldn't even feed my teenage stomach. How was it going to feed all these families?*

I gave them the basket and the remarkable happened. As they'd passed it around, each person pulled out a piece of fish and some bread. Some even took two pieces. When the basket returned back to me, there was actually more in it than when it first started. I looked into the basket and then up at Jesus and then back into the basket.

"Pass it around." Jesus had smiled as he saw my confused look. "Keep passing it around."

I had moved to another group of people and once again gave them the basket. After we had fed all the groups Jesus asked for us to go around to see if anyone was still hungry. It had been a long day and many people were still hungry. After everyone was finished we came back to him, each with a basket in hand. Each of the baskets was nearly full. He had provided when there wasn't anything to provide.

Shaking off the memory, I said, "Actually, we didn't pay for this food," correcting Peter with a look of disdain. "It was given to us, so if anyone can get upset, it's the owner of this home."

"Where is the owner?" Thomas asked through a yawn while stretching his arms.

"I thought you all saw him yesterday and asked for a place of refuge," Peter said astonished.

The group of brothers all shook their head in the daylight. None of them had seen the owner yesterday.

"Are we trespassing?" I asked in trepidation, looking each of my brothers in their eyes for the first time since we were in this room two nights ago.

"I'll find out," Thomas said getting up and heading downstairs to walk around to the home's entrance.

I looked around the room that seemed drastically different in the daylight. It was warm and homey, whereas last night it felt like a cavernous dungeon.

Light always made things better. Always.

"I'm sorry, John," Peter said, apologizing after a few minutes of pacing along the wall away from the window. "I'm just trying to look out for everyone."

"I know," I said. "But it's going to be okay. If we need anything we have ways of getting it. That man didn't."

Peter couldn't disagree. His vision was tunneling into a darkness where he couldn't see any good or hope. He knew I was right. He nodded his head as if remembering when Jesus fed the large groups of people just as I did.

"We are going to be okay," I said with a smile as I exited the room and headed down the stairs.

"Find him?" I asked Thomas as he was walking back up.

"No. I have no idea where he is."

"Well, I'm going to go check on Mary. Want to join me?"

"Are you sure it's safe?" Thomas asked apprehensively.

Chapter 48

Thomas

"Are you sure it's safe?" I asked, standing on the bottom step as if it was the invisible boundary between safety and vulnerability.

"Thomas, you can stay if you don't feel like going," John said compassionately. "I'll be back later."

John may have been the youngest in the group, but it seemed like he had something he could teach the rest of us.

"No, I'm coming," I said letting my foot dangle off the step and hit the solid ground. "Do the others know?"

"I told Peter earlier I was going," John said as we stepped out of the shadows into the sunlight. The sky was overcast with very little blue showing. Even though it was daytime, it didn't feel like a normal day. The morning fog hadn't lifted, causing the alleys to look more menacing than normal. "How are you doing?" he asked as I watched the surroundings. Even though he felt comfortable walking the streets, I still had an uneasiness about being seen.

"I feel like I'm in a fog," I said seeing two figures coming towards us from the opposite direction. I quickly turned my head and lifted my hand to hide my face.

"Thomas, if you didn't want to come, you didn't have to," he said encouragingly. "Really."

"No," I said straightening myself up after the pair passed. "I was thinking about Mary all day yesterday. I hated myself for not being there for her, but..." I didn't want to finish my sentence. It would show my true colors, and I wasn't ready to describe myself in that way just yet.

"She understands," John said walking a little more briskly than he had a few minutes before.

"You don't have to walk so fast," I said trying to keep up. "Won't that look suspicious?"

John looked over at me and smiled as he slowed his pace.

"What do you think about Peter's plan?" he asked in a hushed voice.

I wanted to ask him the same question. I wanted to hear someone else's opinion on the matter. "I don't know, but I'm afraid he's going to rush and do something stupid. What about you?"

"I think the whole plan is senseless," he said defiantly. "Look at us," he stopped and scanned his head over his body. "Do I look like I could take on one of those guards? They have been fighting and killing for years and they would break me in one swift swoop."

"Why didn't you say something?" I asked as I looked down at my skinny arms and knew John and I were not much different.

John eyed me suspiciously. "Why didn't *you*?"

I deserved that remark.

"So, do you think anyone is on Peter's side?" I asked softly to not be heard by any of the homes we were passing.

"I think if Peter says to go, many of them will go," he said making another turn down a busier road.

"Can we stay on some of the quieter roads?" I asked. He agreed and we snuck across the street to continue to walk in the more shadowed alleys where clothes hung damp from the storm overhead.

"So what are your plans now?" John asked casually.

"For what?"

"For the future," he said with a saddened tone in his voice. "Whatever future that may be."

I had heard some of the others talking yesterday about their possible futures, but I wasn't ready to think of the coming days. I wasn't even ready to think of the coming hours. I didn't answer and he didn't ask again. I think we both realized we were in the middle of a crossroads and there wasn't a good feeling on which direction to take.

"Just a couple more turns," he said as he led the way.

I had been to Mary's a few times, but I didn't have the route memorized. I especially wouldn't know how to get there from where we were hiding.

"So, do you believe Jesus was anything special, or was he just a con?" I asked in a defeated tone. I didn't want to believe he was a fraud, but the way the last day had spun out of control, I couldn't see it any other way.

"Oh no," John said with a blank stare fixing his eyes ahead of him. "He was special." He stopped and squinted his eyes. "Let's turn back and hide."

There were four Roman guards heading our way and they didn't seem like they were bundles of joy this morning.

"Can you believe that?" we heard one of the Roman guards say as they passed where we were hidden. "Shifts to guard a dead man's tomb? What are they going to want us do next, bow down to the man?"

The soldiers laughed at the comment as they marched through the damp streets. Another soldier said a snide remark and the voices trailed off into the distance.

"You don't think they're talking about...?" By his nod, I figured John was thinking the same thing.

"What is going on?" John asked as he sunk further into the shadows. He sat down and rested his hands on the ground, jumping as he looked at what his hand just touched. It was a leg. "Who's that?"

I stood up and leaned over the sleeping man and noticed that he wasn't sleeping from the bloodstain and hole in his chest. "Is that...?"

John jumped to his feet and ran. I wasn't as fast as John, but I was right on his tail. He was dodging through the alleys at full speed when he finally jumped into a house. I followed, just a few seconds behind him.

"John! Thomas!" Mary Magdalene said shockingly as we both heaved trying to gain some breath into our lungs. "Why were you running?"

"There's a...there's a...." John tried to say but couldn't get the words out through his short breaths.

"Body. A dead body," I finished as I took a seat on the ground, resting my head against the wall.

"It was Barabbas," John said on hinge.

"That was Barabbas?" I asked in shock. "He was the one that..." I started to say as Mary, Jesus' mother, walked into the room. "I'm sorry," was all I could get out before she rushed to my side and hugged me.

Mary Magdalene leaned over and whispered in John's ear.

"We need to talk."

Chapter 49

Mary Magdalene

"We need to talk," I whispered in John's ear, pulling him away from Mary and Thomas. I wanted them to have time alone without prying eyes watching their every move. And I wanted to find out what happened after I left last night.

We walked into another room to have some privacy because I didn't want Mary to hear a word of what Peter was planning.

"So, what was said last night?"

John closed his eyes and shook his head. I could read his body language and knew I wasn't going to want to hear it and he didn't want to say it. "He didn't say anything about you."

"I'm not talking about that," I said scolding him. "I meant about Peter's plan."

"Mary, he's talking crazy," John resigned. I saw the remorse and dread on his face with the possible scheme Peter was instigating. "And the crazier thing is some of them were agreeing with him."

"Are you shocked by that?" I asked astonished. "You teenagers would walk to Egypt if Peter suggested it."

"What are you trying to say?" John asked with an attitude.

"Boys don't always think of the consequences," I said playfully as I hugged him. I wanted him to know I loved him despite the foolish things he had done in the past. "It's just a right of passage, I guess."

"This passage is going to get some of them killed," John said depressingly.

"Yes, but they are thinking what they are doing is right. Peter always thinks he is right," I said as my mind drifted to a happier, safer time when Jesus was teaching.

Jesus had been sharing a message on how the Son of Man must suffer and be rejected and killed. Peter was irate with that message. Peter took Jesus aside and began to rebuke him. Jesus had looked at the people who were around and turned it back on Peter.

"Get behind me, Satan! For you are not setting your mind on the things of God, but on the things of man."

Peter had stood frozen. It was one thing to see Jesus marginalize the Pharisees, but it was another thing to have those words directed at him.

Jesus walked away from Peter and started teaching again, but he kept his eyes on Peter the whole time, as if giving a message just for him. "If anyone would come after me, let him deny himself and take up his cross and follow me. For whoever would save his life will lose it, but whoever loses his life for my sake and the gospel's will save it. For what does it profit a man to gain the whole world and forfeit his soul? For what can a man give in return for his soul?"

Those words started to haunt my soul at how relevant they were today. "John, we have to change their mind," I said desperately. But then another disheartening thought stampeded into my mind. *If Peter wouldn't listen to me last night, why would he listen to me today?*

I let that thought resonate, but I knew John wouldn't be able to sway an entire group. Even though John had attributes they each wished they had, they weren't going to humble themselves and submit to his opinion either.

"So, when are they planning to attack?" I asked, knowing it wouldn't be today since it was the Sabbath.

"I don't know the exact time, but it's going to be soon," he said solemnly.

"Like how soon? They will need a few days to plan their murderous raid."

"Oh, no. It's not going to be days," John said shaking his head. "Peter said something about going at sundown and searching for him."

"Sundown?" I said almost shrieking at the speed of this horrible mistake.

John just nodded his head.

"Him?" I asked. "Who's 'him'?"

John shrugged his shoulders. "He wouldn't tell us his name. It was just one of the guards. He's the first target."

"Peter is going to hunt down one of the guards?" I asked stupefied. "Why that one? I would think he would just wait and surprise attack any guard that came around at the moment they were ready to fight."

John once again shook his head no. "He wants to kill this man first." He stopped and took a deep breath. "He was the guard who crucified Jesus." John bowed his head and I could tell he didn't sleep much last night. He looked scared and tired, and that was not a good combination. "He wants him to pay first. Then they will go after the others. One by one."

Chapter 50

John

"Then they will go after the others." I stopped and shuddered at the chaos that would ensue as a result. "One by one."

Mary poked her head out of the room and peered over at Thomas. "What does he think?"

I thought for a second and knew he was undecided. "I think he's like us; but like you said, I think he could be swayed just to be part of the crowd."

"We need to get him into our circle before Peter gets him into his," she said strategically. "Because once he picks a side, it's going to be hard for him to cross over the line to the other side."

"This just doesn't feel right," I said leaning against the wall. All the strategizing felt like manipulation on both sides. "Why can't this just be over?" I said pitying myself. "It will all be better once it is all over," I said naively.

"And when is that going to be?" Mary asked. "When you all are dead or when they are?" She moved back into the room and leaned against the wall with me. We both slid our bodies down until we were sitting with our knees to our chests. "It's not ever going to be better," she said looking off into the distance. "It's never going to be better."

I closed my eyes and tried to let my mind settle from this deep, stressful conversation as a memory from two nights ago stilled my nerves.

"Do you now believe?" Jesus had asked as we were reclining after the Passover meal. He had been talking about random topics when suddenly, it was like a match was struck and we started to see things in the light.

"Behold, the hour is coming, indeed it has come, when you will be scattered, each to his own home, and will leave me alone. Yet I am not alone, for the Father is with me. I have said these things to you, that in me you may have peace. In the world you will have tribulation. But take heart; I have overcome the world."

With the memory of his words, my breathing started to slow to a light, restful one. I felt like Jesus was right there with me in that room, just as he was with me two nights ago. I let his words pour over me, because in this moment of uncertainty, I needed some assurance. I needed his firm assertion he had overcome the world. I needed that encouragement that even though we had scattered, we could unite as one.

"Mary," I said opening my eyes and looking over.

But she was sleeping. I understood her exhaustion, but something had come over me. I quietly stood up and stepped over her legs and exited the room. I found Mary and Thomas sitting at the table talking, and I knew I needed to start bringing some peace. There was too much hate and division right now and it was going to fester and tear us more apart.

Even though I wasn't happy with what happened to my friend and teacher, I wasn't happy with what Peter was pursuing either.

I sat down beside Thomas, and Mary asked about Mary Magdalene. I told her she was sleeping in the other room. She quickly grabbed a blanket from the corner and went to cover her.

"I have a question to ask," I said when Mary walked out of earshot. "And we need your help."

"What is it?"

Chapter 51

Thomas

"What is it?" I asked, feeling needed and important.

"We need you to agree with us that Peter's plan isn't a good one," John whispered, keeping a watch if Mary walked back into the room.

"Okay," I said getting a little caught off guard. Over everything that had happened over the last few days, I was surprised that this was what John was getting nervous about. Peter's little plan. Maybe it was sitting with Jesus' mother, but Peter's conversation was the furthest thing from my mind.

"I'm serious," John reiterated defensively. "You have to listen to me."

"Maybe Peter was just upset and letting off a little steam," I said. "I mean, maybe this was his way of grieving."

"I've seen Peter when he was grieving, and this is not typical Peter," John rebutted.

I knew what he meant. We had each had moments in the last three years when we grieved in various ways. Seeing loved ones get sick, hearing news of bad things that had happened while we were traveling to villages with Jesus, or even seeing friends die. I would never forget the moment when Jesus told us Lazarus had died.

"Let us also go, that we may die with him," I had said to the other disciples and we all joined Jesus on the journey.

As we were walking to Bethany someone had said to Jesus, "Rabbi, the Jews were just now seeking to stone you, and are you

173

going there again?" It was a reasonable question, and I remember wondering the same thing.

But Jesus wasn't concerned.

"Are there not twelve hours in the day? If someone walks in the day, he does not stumble, because he sees the light of this world. But if anyone walks in the night, he stumbles, because the light is not in him."

When we'd finally arrived, Lazarus' sister Martha seized Jesus. "Lord, if you had been here, my brother would not have died."

I remembered looking over at Peter who was quiet with emotions. He wasn't cursing or screaming in rage at the passing of Lazarus. No, he was calm and reserved, but I saw a tear escape.

But then Jesus had said something strange, taking the moment to teach.

"I am the resurrection and the life. Whoever believes in me, though he die, yet shall he live, and everyone who lives and believes in me shall never die. Do you believe this?"

We had all nodded in agreement. I usually just agreed with what Jesus said whether I understood him or not. I had quickly learned he was always right, so why oppose him?

"Where have you laid him?" Jesus had asked Martha and Mary, his other sister. When they took us to his tomb, I'd watched Jesus cry for his friend.

My heart sank for him as Martha's earlier accusation finally registered. *Lord, if you had been here, my brother would not have died.*

I surveyed the area and everyone was weeping for this man. I hadn't known Lazarus very well, but I too started to shed a few tears.

Maybe it hit me that Jesus wasn't always right. If he had let his beloved friend Lazarus die, then would he always be there to protect me? I wondered if the others were thinking the same thing. Doubt started to creep into my mind questioning who Jesus really was.

Then Jesus asked for them to open Lazarus' tomb.

My stomach had started to knot at the thought of them opening a tomb holding a dead body. I had seen dead bodies before, some decomposing on the side of the road I traveled with my parents as a kid. My mother would ask me to turn my head and not look, but I always had to look to figure out where the horrible smell was coming from.

As the tomb opened, I took a deep breath and held it. I wasn't ready to be smacked with that disgusting aroma. But my breath was stolen another way.

"Lazarus, come out!" Jesus had cried with a loud booming voice.

Suddenly, a man bound from head to toe in linen strips walked out. He was hobbling and I couldn't believe my eyes. He was a dead man walking.

"Unbind him, and let him go," Jesus had said enthusiastically. "Let him go."

I had looked over, inhaling deeply and breathing the sweet aroma of frankincense and saw Peter beaming a bright smile. His mourning had passed. He was joyous again.

I wanted to see his joy again now.

"So, what do you suggest," I asked John. "If we all turn against him won't that make him feel betrayed? But encouraging him will only cause doom in the end."

"We have to get him to convince himself this isn't a good idea," John smiled optimistically. "We have to do this to keep the group intact. We have to do this for Jesus."

"By the way you are smiling, you have a plan?" I grinned. It felt good to smile after the last couple of days of hiding in silence.

"Not a clue," John softly chuckled. "Not a single clue."

Chapter 52

John

"Not a single clue," I said. I laughed at the notion everything was hanging on this one moment. If we failed, we would probably all die, because if Peter went after some of the soldiers, they would eventually track us all down even if we didn't fight with him. If we won, well, it wouldn't bring our friend back to life. We would still be without Jesus. So I didn't know what the win would be.

Living the rest of my life knowing Jesus died without a reason wasn't a life I wanted to live. I wanted to live knowing Jesus reigned on his throne and brought the Jews out of bondage. I guess I could live in a dream world where everything was perfect, but then that would lead to many other problems. Self-denial. Isolation. Delusions.

No, that wasn't how Jesus wanted me to live either.

Memories of Jesus kept flooding my mind. Memories of good times we had as we traveled. But mostly, the things I recalled were the words he spoke the night before his death.

"Let not your hearts be troubled. Believe in God; believe in me. In my Father's house are many rooms. If it were not so, would I have told you that I go to prepare a place for you?" When Jesus said these words, my heart had leaped for joy.

A house? A house with many rooms? He was going to restore the kingdom and we were going to take over the palace. I would never have to share a room with my brothers again. I would have a room to myself. For the last three years of traveling from town to town, there were many nights we slept under the stars. But the luxury of having a mansion where we would all live brought life to my bones. It brought a smile to my face as I looked around the room this Passover night. It was a lovely thought to have all my brothers nearby.

"And if I go and prepare a place for you, I will come again and will take you to myself, that where I am you may also be." Jesus had stopped and looked around the dimly lit room with flickering candles as we reclined around the table. "And you know the way to where I am going."

Thomas had quickly asked the question I was thinking. "Lord, we do not know where you are going. How can we know the way?"

I'd nodded my head in agreement because I wondered if I had fallen asleep one night when he told us where to meet him. Was there a secret map we had to find? Was there a hidden hole in the wall we had to know about to get to this mysterious place?

"I am the way, and the truth, and the light. No one comes to the Father except through me. If you had known me, you would have known my Father also. From now on you do know him and have seen him."

I had watched in awe as he spoke. I didn't have any idea where he was going or how I would get there, but he promised I would be there. I had looked around the room and assumed that someone else knew and they would lead me to him. Probably Peter as he was the oldest and knew the most.

"Whatever you ask in my name, this I will do, that the Father may be glorified in the Son. If you ask me anything in my name, I will do it." Jesus had stopped and looked at each one of us.

I had waited for someone to ask him another question, but no one did. I didn't want to look like the dumb young one, so I'd stayed silent. I looked over at Peter who smiled back at me. I knew Peter would always be by my side and would help me find this place Jesus was talking about.

I looked over at Thomas as we sat in Mary's house and realized I couldn't always blindly follow Peter. I needed God to direct us.

"We need to pray," I said seriously.

"Okay," he said nonchalantly.

"No, I mean, we need to *pray*," I said as emphatically as I could, widening my eyes to show how important this conversation was to me.

He repeated, "Okay," as he widened his eyes back at me.

"You're not getting it," I moaned.

"No, I'm not," he said shaking his head.

"Jesus said we need…" I started as Jude, Jesus' brother, walked into the home. I stopped talking because I knew he wouldn't want to hear from me.

"Go on, John, what were you saying?" Jude asked with a smug smile. "What did good ol' Jesus say? Bet he's not talking to you now."

Chapter 53

Jude

"What did good ol' Jesus say? Bet he's not talking to you now," I said with a sadistic laugh. Yes, I knew it wasn't in good taste, but I was tired of hearing all this talk about my stupid brother. I thought by now, they would stop acting like he was something special. He wasn't anything special. He died just like everyone else.

"Jude, please," John begged, craning his neck to look around. "Your mom is in the next room."

"She knows how I feel," I said annoyed. "She's always known and never cared."

"I think she cares that you are so vocal about your hatred," Thomas spoke up. "Jesus never said an unkind word to you."

"You don't know the real Jesus," I retorted, rolling my eyes at the brainwashed teens before me.

"Fine, tell us, who was the real Jesus?" Thomas asked agitatedly.

"For starters, a liar," I began. I had a lifetime of things I could say about Jesus. A lifetime. "Oh, don't get me wrong, he was a good storyteller. I can't deny that. But his stories always showcased him being something greater than everyone else. And if you look at him now," I stopped and leaned down, looking into their eyes, "he's no greater than one of those street performers begging for spare change."

I watched their faces sink at my words. They didn't comment. Not one word. They just stared at me with distaste as if sucking on a lemon. Yes, my words may have been sour and not full of false hope and rainbows of a coming kingdom, but they were from a lifetime of watching Jesus.

I had asked myself a few times in the last day, *Will I miss him?* There was a part of me that loved him. We were brothers. I couldn't forget the good times we had as kids. He loved me. I know he did, but there was always something different about him than the rest of us. All my brothers and sisters would see it. Even the rest of the town saw it because I heard him say one time, "A prophet is not without honor, except in his hometown and among his relatives and in his own household." He was talking directly to me when he said that. That was when he started traveling to nearby villages and towns preaching. I guess I forced him to leave.

Thomas and John didn't ask for any more examples of Jesus' charade life. I think they started to see the writing on the wall. It pained me to burst their bubble, but sometimes people need to be shocked into awareness.

I walked away and left them sitting wide-eyed and found my mother lying on the floor beside a sleeping woman. I didn't want to disturb either of them. Some may have thought I was cruel and heartless, but I wasn't jaded. I was just a realist.

I saw Jesus for who he was before anyone else did.

What happened yesterday should have never happened. But I couldn't say I didn't see it coming. Getting a following like he did with the crowd he did said a lot about him. I didn't mean to judge, but when he hung around delinquents, a good reputation wasn't going to follow. Even he couldn't make manure smell like a rose. And he couldn't clean up a tax collector's past with a kind word.

He just couldn't.

I looked down at my mother and felt sad for her delusion. She also didn't have the best reputation. Yes, she was loving and the best mother I could ask for, but she made up a story about being pregnant with Jesus as a virgin. I just couldn't forget that. That story must have been derived from a bitter place in her history. And for Dad to agree to it. I could never understand that both of them clung to this lie, even to his death.

They didn't talk about it much. I couldn't remember the last time she mentioned it, but I'd seen how the people still looked at her. They all knew the story she created. And none of them believed it. Thirty years later, she was still mocked behind her back.

And she didn't even know.

That was what saddened me the most. But in my lowest of moments, I had a horrible thought. Maybe Jesus got the idea he was someone sent by God to save us from her. What if it wasn't my brother's fault he acted like he did? Maybe she'd trained him to be how he was.

But as quickly as I would think those thoughts I would have to shake them out of my head. Every time I thought it, I lost a little bit of respect for my mother. And I loved my mother too much to think those thoughts about her.

I stood outside the room and watched my mother sleep. In these moments, I couldn't see anything but love for her. These were the moments I wanted to remember. These were the times I wanted to store away in my memories. When my love for my mother outweighed all my nagging thoughts.

When I heard a rustling in the room, I poked my head in and found Mary opening her eyes. She quietly got up and covered my mother with the blanket she'd had on her.

She tiptoed out of the room and smiled at me, but we didn't say a word. We waited until we got back into the main room.

"Hey Jude."

Chapter 54

Mary Magdalene

"Hey Jude," I softly said as I yawned, sitting down beside John and Thomas. I needed that little nap, and I knew Mary needed to rest much more than I did. "We are about to leave. Can you stay here to be with your mom? Some of the women are going to be over soon, but I don't want to leave her alone."

"Of course," Jude smiled as he sat down as well.

I looked over at John and Thomas, but something was different about them. I looked over at Jude questioningly and he shrugged his shoulders.

I didn't believe his shrug for a second. I knew he had something to do with it.

"Come on," I said standing up, snapping my fingers in front of John's face. He shook his head as if waking up from a trance. "We need to leave."

"Where are we going?" John asked as he and Thomas stood up and followed me to the door.

I didn't want to talk in front of Jude. I knew he had a way of twisting everything about Jesus. I had seen his cynical side many times, and Mary had warned me about her children's attitudes toward Jesus. Even though they were his brothers and sisters, they'd treated Jesus like he wasn't even related to them during the last three years.

"Mary, where are we going?" Thomas asked as they followed closely behind me. I wasn't old enough to be their mother, but I was old enough to be a protective older sister to them.

"Back to see the others," I said defiantly. "We have to stop this madness before it escalates."

The city streets were pretty quiet since it was the Sabbath and the majority of the town was at temple today. I hardly ever missed going to the temple, but I didn't feel like going today. I didn't know if I could take seeing the faces of the men and women who'd demanded Jesus be killed yesterday. I was glad the city streets were empty. I wasn't ready to come face to face with anyone just yet.

We turned a corner, but John grabbed my shoulder. "Not there," he said.

Suddenly, I remembered what he and Thomas had said when they came running into Mary's, but I hadn't asked him about it. I didn't want to go back to that moment from last night. As we continued to walk straight I couldn't help but turn my head.

I could have died in that alleyway.

All my life I had had respect for the Roman government, not from my own thoughts but from one of oppression. The kind of respect slaves had for their owners: if they followed their orders, they would live a more peaceful life than if they tried to defy them. That had been my whole existence.

Until last night.

Last night I saw a different side of the Roman guards.

Yes, they were cruel, able to kill on the spot without a hesitation or second thought, which scared me a little. But I also saw the look on that one soldier's face who saved me, Longinus. It was a look of concern. He'd walked me back to Mary's when he could have left me to fend for myself. He'd protected me when no one else would. Even if I had screamed out last night, I wasn't sure anyone would have come to my rescue.

Technically it was the Sabbath and many would have seen fighting off a killer as a sin on a holy day. Even to save me, they would have thought it would be better to watch me die than lift a finger to harm another person.

But not Jesus. Jesus would have helped.

I turned my head back to see up the road when a man looked at me and smiled. I had seen the man before, but I couldn't remember where.

"Good day," he greeted us warmly.

Chapter 55
Unnamed Man

"Good day," I said smiling to three people. I was trying to convince myself it was a good day, even after the massacre I'd witnessed the day before. After the depressing blow of yesterday, I needed to find some joy. I loved seeing the faces of people as I walked the city road, but today was a harder day than most.

I recalled a time I was lying outside the temple where many of the sick and lame begged day and night for some compassion, encouragement, and food. It was sad when people had so much, yet they couldn't offer a little selfless love to help someone in need. But I was used to it. Even my own family wouldn't help. I was despised because my disability shone unfavorably on them as well.

As I child, I would often hear my mother crying. I would walk up to her and rub her cheeks, and she would hug me in the confines of our home. But when we were out in public, she wouldn't even hold my hand. That was a sad life as a little boy, to be loved in secret, but not allowed to share it with the world.

I remembered one day, a group of us were huddled, pleading for some money to buy some food when I heard some men heading our way.

"Rabbi, who sinned, this man or his parents, that he was born blind?" one of the voices asked.

I had lowered my head in shame. This was my life. People didn't talk to me. They talked about me. Even though I couldn't see their cruel eyes, I felt their downcast looks. I heard the disdain in their voices. I felt the patting of their feet in judgment on the ground.

Another voice answered, sounding like he had more years on him than the other. "It was not that this man sinned, or his parents, but that the works of God might be displayed in him. We must work the works of him who sent me while it is day; night is coming, when no one can work. As long as I am in the world, I am the light of the world."

I had listened with intrigue. I hadn't felt hatred and disgrace as this man spoke about me. He hadn't scorned my mother for her sins or said it was my fault. All my life I had been pleading for God to show me what I did to deserve my blindness. But all I could ever see was the darkness, as if God wasn't even listening to my prayers. My parents had given up. They couldn't live with the shame I placed on them, so I had to beg for my existence. It was a sad life knowing even my family ignored me when they walked by.

I knew my mother's scent by her oils and lotions. That mixture of aloe and lavender brought both a warmth and a coldness to my heart, because I could smell it coming and then I could smell it leave. I used to call out her name, and I knew it was her because the footsteps would stop.

But they didn't even stop anymore.

Suddenly, I felt a man put something slimy on my eyes. I'd thought, *What a cruel joke*. I had thought he was a kind man, but he was just playing with me. It seemed I would always be a laughingstock.

"Go, wash in the pool of Siloam," he had said with conviction.

I'd raised my head and let him look upon my face. Tears were streaming down my cheeks. I wanted my tears to wash away the gunk he had placed over my eyes, but it was too thick. My tears wouldn't even come close to cleansing all he placed in them.

I had stood and walked to the pool of Siloam. I'd wanted to dive headfirst into the water and drown from the embarrassment, but my suicide would only put a greater shame on my family.

With trembling hands, I reached down into the cool water and lifted a handful of refreshment and started cleaning my eyes. I repeated the process until my eyes were rid of whatever he placed on them. I blinked my eyelids to get everything out, when suddenly, streaks of light shined every time I opened them.

As I splashed more and more water onto my face, the blurry images started to still. I began seeing precise objects. I lifted my hands and felt a hairy cheek as I saw my hand feel my face in the water's reflection. I stared at my own image amazed. After a lifetime of not knowing who I was, I finally saw myself.

My insides heaved at what I just realized. My blindness was gone. My shame had vanished. My lifetime of being looked down on was a distant memory.

I didn't want to leave the pool because I was so mesmerized with my own reflection. I had spent years wondering how I looked based on my touch, but I couldn't get past the details I couldn't feel. The color of my hair, the brightness of my twinkling eyes, the warmth of my smile. I couldn't remember the last time I'd smiled. But I was feeling it and seeing it for the first time.

I jumped up from the pool and ran back to where I had been sitting. I was screaming and shouting; people who apparently knew me started talking among themselves.

"You're not that man who was blind, are you?" someone had asked as I went running back to the temple.

"I am! I am that man!" I'd screamed for joy. "But now I can see! Now I can see!"

My healing had become the talk of the area. Some of the Pharisees even came to question me. I was expecting a hug or excitement at the miracle, but that wasn't what happened.

They started questioning me. They kept asking me to retell the story of what happened as if the last twenty-five years of my life had been a lie and I had merely pretended to be a blind beggar.

"This man is not from God, for he does not keep the Sabbath," one of the priests had said with condemnation.

My heart sunk. My years of blindness were over and I could finally see the world. I could also see things I didn't want to see, like their looks of judgment. All my life I had heard their voices as they would talk to me, but I never saw their looks.

Their expressions stung more than all the rude words they'd ever said.

They asked for my parents to come and confirm the story. They agreed I was born blind, but they didn't know how my sight returned. My father had interrupted my mother from speaking. "Ask him; he is of age. He will speak for himself."

My mother wouldn't even look at me. She'd kept her eyes glued to her feet. She was fearful of the men whom she stood before. If she or my father said anything wrong they would quickly be thrown out of the synagogue and asked to never return. So they were silent. Even still, after all these years they wouldn't defend me.

That thought had hurt, but I didn't let my mother's displaced eyes steal my joy.

The priests had even tried to trick me with their questions.

"Give glory to God. We know that this man is a sinner," one of the priests said, speaking of the man who opened my eyes to see.

I looked around at everyone judging and watching me. All my life I had been ignored, but for the first time in my life, I was being listened to. "Whether he is a sinner I do not know. One thing I do know, that though I was blind, now I see," I'd said with the biggest smile I had ever worn. It seemed like my smile continued to grow larger and larger, as if reminding myself to not let these men steal my joy.

They once again asked what this stranger, Jesus, did to me.

"I have told you already, and you would not listen. Why do you want to hear it again? Do you also want to become his disciples?" I had asked. I knew it wasn't smart to mock them, but I was flabbergasted by their concern for this man. He wasn't an evil man. He was a kind man who did what no one else had ever done for me before. He had stooped down and touched me. Even if I didn't get my sight back, he had spoken words of kindness over me. Words I had never heard said about me.

"Why, this is an amazing thing! You do not know where he comes from, and yet he opened my eyes. We know that God does not listen to sinners, but if anyone is a worshipper of God and does his will, God listens to him. Never since the world began has it been heard that anyone opened the eyes of a man born blind. If this man were not from God, he could do nothing," I'd said with hope and stamina. I wasn't going to let their words hurt me anymore.

"You were born in utter sin, and would you teach us?" one of the priests had shouted.

I had looked over and saw my mother tremble. I ran over to her and hugged her and my father. "This is not your fault! Neither of you did anything wrong!" I'd said as my mother finally looked up into my eyes. Tears were falling down her cheeks. "You did nothing wrong," I said repeatedly, kissing her cheeks. "I love you both, so much."

"Get them out of here!" one of the priests had commanded, and we left the temple for the first time as a family.

"I'm proud of you, son," my father had said, hugging my shoulder. "I'm sor..." he started to say, but I stopped him.

"I love you both," I'd interrupted. I didn't want them to live with guilt for the last years. I wanted to start fresh, just like my vision.

I had been walking with my parents who were taking me back to their home, the home I hadn't stepped in for many years, when a familiar voice was behind me.

"Do you believe in the Son of Man?" the man who'd healed me asked.

"And who is he, sir, that I may believe in him?" I asked as my parents left me outside.

"You have seen him, and it is he who is speaking to you," Jesus had said with a smile.

"Lord, I believe." I bowed down and kissed his feet. I wept for the healing I had received, both physical and emotional. I had my sight renewed and my relationship with my family mended. I looked up and knew I was looking at the Son of Man. I was looking at the savior of the world.

Who else could make a blind man's eyes see?

Now, the day after that great man's execution, I was on the same street. "Good day to you too," the young boy said to me as he passed.

I hoped that it would get better. That was all I had – hope. But I would forever be thankful for Jesus and how I went from being a blind man to a happy one.

Chapter 56
John

"Good day to you too," I said, thinking his smile didn't seem real, but forced. As if trying to convince himself. I could commiserate. But unlike him, I wasn't trying to tell myself it was a good day. I knew it wasn't going to be a good one.

We were on our way back to the home the others were hiding in, when I spotted a familiar set of eyes and head of hair. He was hiding behind a tower of empty woven baskets needing to be filled with goods to sell at the market tomorrow.

"Matthew?" I said, quickly making our way to his little hiding place.

He was startled and didn't rise, but sunk lower, hoping to be unnoticed by anyone else who may be passing by.

"Shhhh," he whispered.

"Why are you hiding here?" Mary asked suspiciously, looking around to see if they were being watched.

"I'm keeping watch on the soldiers," he said softly.

"Why?" I asked baffled.

"Will you stop talking so loudly?" he quietly begged.

"If you're trying to hide, I spotted you," I scoffed. "And they will too."

"Why are you keeping watch?" Thomas asked, gaining a little bravery after seeing his friend huddled beside a family of rats.

"Peter asked us to," Matthew said, stretching his neck up to look around at the surroundings and check for Roman guards.

"Who's 'us'?" Mary asked, walking to the middle of the road to look up and down to see if she could see another one of her brothers hiding in the shadows.

"A few of us are scattered around the city, trying to keep track of where the guards are."

"Why?" I asked as Mary returned to us, shaking her head to show she didn't see anyone else.

"So we can alert the others if it looks like they are coming for us," Matthew said wearily.

His tone of voice told me he was frightened. The look in his eyes told me he was scared. The way he hid himself from us told me he was petrified. But here he was hiding behind a stack of baskets doing as he was commanded.

That scared me more than what the guards were going to do to me.

If Matthew had fallen into the blind following of Peter, even if he didn't want to, that meant the others probably did too. If they each were following Peter, it was going to be hard to try to sway Peter from doing anything rash or foolish.

"Is everyone hiding around the streets, or are some of them hiding in the upper room?" Mary asked. It came across harshly, but we all knew what she meant.

"About half and half," Matthew answered as he rearranged his wall of baskets to better hide himself from the rest of the prying eyes possibly lurking around every corner in Jerusalem. The town had never been peaceful since the Roman occupation. Roman guards and the citizens of Jerusalem had always clashed over the cultural differences.

We each thought the other was wrong, but since they were in charge, we had to bend some to their thinking, which didn't go over well in some households.

I looked up at the cloudy sky, wondering when the sun's rays were going to shine down to give us some relief from the depressing gray skyline. I longed for the clouds to part. I knew it wouldn't solve all our problems, but it would at least bring a little warmth to an otherwise dreary day.

We quietly said goodbye and walked away. As we passed, I remembered one of Jesus' teachings. It had been a beautiful day about three years ago. Crowds had gathered around and Jesus climbed up on a hillside to be seen by all who came to listen to him.

"You are the light of the world. A city set on a hill cannot be hidden. Nor do people light a lamp and put it under a basket, but on a stand, and it gives light to all in the house. In the same way, let your light shine before others, so that they may see your good works and give glory to your Father who is in Heaven," he said. He'd stopped and let that message sink in and then continued with many more teachings on that day.

It was day I would never forget as his well of wisdom seemed to be without limit. Each time he'd spoken, his words watered my soul like a cool waterfall of grace. I needed that now.

I looked back and saw Matthew hiding behind the baskets and my heart sunk. He wasn't living for his light to shine. No, he was hiding behind a basket like Jesus warned us.

Earlier in Jesus' teachings that day, he'd stated various oxymorons. When he first said them, I was confused, but as I was walking, they started coming into my ears loud and clear – making perfect sense.

I started to recite them verbatim.

"Blessed are the poor in spirit for theirs is the kingdom of heaven," I said softly.

"What did you say, John?" Mary asked, leaning over to hear my words.

"Blessed are those who mourn, for they shall be comforted," I continued as Thomas, too, started to lean in to hear what I was saying.

"Blessed are the meek, for they shall inherit the earth. Blessed are those who hunger and thirst for righteousness, for they shall be satisfied. Blessed are the merciful, for they shall receive mercy. Blessed are the pure in heart, for they shall see God. Blessed are the peacemakers, for they shall be called sons of God."

"And daughters," chimed in Mary with a smile.

The gloomy clouds slowly started to part and I could feel a singular ray of light beaming down on us from above.

"Blessed are those who are persecuted for righteousness' sake, for theirs is the kingdom of heaven. Blessed are you when others revile you and persecute you and utter all kinds of evil against you falsely on my account. Rejoice and be glad, for your reward is great in heaven, for so they persecuted the prophets who were before you," I said as we came to the home where our friends were hiding.

"That was beautiful," Mary said as she was about to step into the passageway beside the house, but I stopped her.

"Those were the words of Jesus," I said as I once again remembered the heavenly day when I first heard them. "I thought Jesus was saying these words for when we have to stand up against our enemies, but what if he was saying those words for this moment?" I stopped and looked at Thomas and Mary. "It's easy to stand up against people who may not care for you, but it's going to be hard to stand up against the people in this room. People who are going to think we are turning our backs on them. They may say some hurtful things. Are you up to it?"

"I would rather be a peacemaker than a war starter," Mary said sincerely as she looked over at Thomas.

Chapter 57
Mary Magdalene

"I would rather be a peacemaker than a war starter," I said, glancing over at Thomas and then John. "You both agree, right?"

John nodded his head while Thomas ignored the question and looked at the door.

"Thomas, you are going to help us, aren't you?" John asked.

I could tell by Thomas' silence that doubt was growing inside him. He couldn't bear to look at John. He slowly blinked and looked up, as if wanting to be anywhere than there.

"It's your decision," I said, knowing it was pointless to try to twist his arm. The main person we needed to convince was Peter. If Peter stopped the charge, then the others would as well. "Come on, boys."

The three of us walked up the stairs together. I wondered who was going to stand together when we got to the top. With each step I dreaded what was waiting at the top, but at the same time, I wanted to run up two at a time to get it over with. I had a twinge of hope combined with a pinch of failure. I wanted us to stand united, but I was afraid we were going to fall divided.

I stepped into the upper room and felt a chill. My mind flashed to a time when Jesus was living and breathing. When he healed the sick and calmed my nerves with just a look.

"Every kingdom divided against itself is laid waste," Jesus had stated moments after healing a demon-oppressed man. "And no city or house divided against itself will stand." He'd looked over at the

Pharisees who were waiting eagerly for Jesus to misspeak, but he never did.

He never did.

"Or how can someone enter a strong man's house and plunder his goods, unless he first binds the strong man? Then indeed he may plunder his house. Whoever is not with me is against me, and whoever does not gather with me scatters."

"What did you say?" Thomas asked as I stepped further into the room. I shook myself awake, not knowing what he was talking about as I felt the darkness wrap around me like a wet blanket. I didn't feel anything soothing in this room. I felt what Jesus had forced out of people many times before. I felt the oppression that was magnifying in the room, growing thicker and heavier each second I stood in the entryway.

"Mary," one of the four said as they sat at the table, huddled over a single candle and a piece of parchment.

Each one raised their heads, and I saw their looks weren't welcoming, but guilty. Caught scheming. Caught planning. Caught formulating a plan that could end in an untimely demise. The fragile flame flickered, dancing the light upon each of their faces. Bartholomew gave me a slight smile. But it was full of discomfort. Andrew looked up and didn't even pretend to smile. He just looked distracted and disjointed. Thaddaeus eyed me suspiciously, as if deciding if I was a backstabber or a comrade. Finally, Peter sat in the middle, huddled over the paper, not lifting his head in my direction.

"Peter," John said from behind me, storming into the room with a ravage tone.

"Wait a second," Peter said annoyed, lifting his hand causing John to stop in his tracks. "We are busy."

Chapter 58
Peter

"We are busy," I said, trying hard to not lose my train of thought. I didn't care what John was barging in to tell us. Unless it pertained to vengeance, I wasn't interested in his meaningless words. And that is what his words most likely were. Meaningless.

I didn't know who else was with them, but I heard a third set of footsteps walking into the room. I didn't care either.

Thaddaeus, Bartholomew, Andrew, and I had devised multiple plans to strategically knock off the Roman guards one at a time. I had five other men lurking around the city, scoping out information. One was at the Roman guards' headquarters, watching from afar. One was outside of the temple listening to worshippers who may have heard some rumors. Two were in various spots on the Roman guards' surveillance route they walked throughout the day. The final and most important one was following the first guard I planned to kill.

And I was going to be the one to kill him.

This morning, I peered my head out the window and saw the man suited in his Roman guard uniform walking the street below, and my blood began to boil. I had to do all I could to not jump out the window and kill him with my bare hands. There was so much pent-up anger. He wouldn't have lasted ten seconds. But that would not have been the wisest course of action. One death was not enough to show them our importance.

We would need much more bloodshed to wound and defeat the tyranny Rome had had over us for too long. We would need much more.

John and Mary were murmuring between themselves, but I didn't care. We had spent the last hour deciding which locations had the best opportunity to attack without being seen or apprehended. We knew that most of the time the guards worked in pairs, so we had decided it would be best to attack as the guards were leaving or returning home. Guards usually didn't walk each other home after a long day. No, they each only cared about themselves.

A smile started to grow under my nose as I looked around the table. The three of them were also smiling at the work we had accomplished. We may not have had the military expertise of the Romans. We may not have had the weaponry or armor. We may not have had the numbers, but what we did have was the determination.

We had the determination to fight until the end.

"So," Thomas said walking up from behind and peering his head between Thaddaeus and myself to look at the paper before him. "You think it can work?"

I looked over at John with his downcast eyes and then up at Thomas with a pair of bright brown eyes. "Definitely."

"Peter, we need to talk," Mary said urgently, as the sound of stomping feet running up the stairs echoed through the room.

"It can wait," I said as the room quickly went from quietly stewing to loudly brewing energy as three of the five spies returned with eager faces and grit.

"No, it can't," she said as I looked away from her and focused all my attention on my men's findings. Scratch that, my men's findings.

"One at a time, men," I said commandingly as I purposely looked at Mary. "One at a time."

They each started telling their opinion on where to attack. As they spoke, I looked at the original three at the table and nodded my head in agreement as I pointed at the map we created. The places the spies were telling us coincided with the places we had already figured were the points of easy kills.

"So, where is James?" I asked, since his finding was the most important. At least for tonight. He was the one I sent out to follow Longinus, the guard who killed Jesus. His report was going to start the unraveling of the Roman hold on Jerusalem. His information was the one I longed for the most.

"I think he's still out," Phillip answered. "I remember seeing him outside of the guard's home when I was coming back. He said he didn't know very much because as soon as the guard got home he went to bed. He said something about the guard being on watch duty somewhere tonight, but he didn't know where yet."

"Watch duty tonight?" I smiled starting to see the plan come together. "If we get him tonight, everything is really going to start tomorrow. Are you ready for this?"

Everyone in the room started cheering, patting each other on the back and enjoying this moment of bonding.

"You need to stop!" Mary shouted from across the room. "Are you seriously going to do this?" she ranted as she started circling the group like a lion prowling a group of antelopes. "Are you really ready to go and fight knowing there is a good chance each of you will be dead by the end of the week? Are you up for that?"

The men didn't say anything, but their looks said it all. They didn't turn to one another for support. They looked to me.

"Yes," I said defiantly. "Yes we are, and there is nothing you can do to stop us!"

"You are talking crazy!" Mary said, eyeing me like I had lost my mind.

But I hadn't lost my mind. For the first time in two days I was finally clear-headed. I had a plan to carry out. I had a reason to keep going, no matter how long I lasted. I had a family to watch out for.

"Men," I said looking at Thaddaeus and Andrew who slowly rose and walked towards the door. "I'm sorry, Mary, but we have to do this."

"But you don't," she said as she looked at me with grieving eyes. "You really don't."

"But we do," Andrew said as he and Thaddaeus stopped and turned, barricading the door with their bodies. "We really do."

Chapter 59
Andrew

"We really do," I said staring at Mary as I inched closer to her.

"What's going on?" she asked, looking around the room as the rest of us formed a circle around the two opposing forces. "Please, stop! Please!" she begged as we continued to move closer, coming within an arm's length of each of them.

"Don't touch me!" John barked as Thaddaeus grabbed him from behind. "Let go!" John yelled as he started maneuvering his body in different directions, trying to free himself from Thaddaeus' strong hands.

"Peter, why?" Mary cried as she fell to the floor, tears gushing from her eyes. Her hands were clawing at the ground as if trying to grip something real. But all she could do was scrape her fingernails along the aged wood. Her tears were causing the golden brown grains to darken a few shades.

I watched as my heart sunk. I suddenly thought, *What are we doing? What has become of us to do this to two of our own?*

But my thoughts flew out of my head as I felt a punch to my jaw. I fell back startled. I wasn't expecting John to break free from Thaddaeus, let alone have enough time to slug me before a few of the others toppled him. I steadied myself as I watched John kick his legs wildly as two of the men held him down on the ground.

"Get off me!" John screamed ferociously, trying his best to break free until another pair of hands held his feet down so he couldn't kick anymore. "Why are you doing this?" he pleaded, looking up into my eyes. "Andrew, why?"

"It's for your own good," I said gingerly. "You will see."

The only part of his body that was free was his head. He looked away and shook his head, staring at the ground two inches from his nose.

"I'm sorry, Mary," he said weakly as he lowered his head to the wooden floor. "I'm so sorry."

Mary didn't respond. She was too shaken to say anything. I leaned down and helped Mary to her feet. She brushed off my assistance and stood up on her own.

"Get the chairs," Peter ordered as Bartholomew and Phillip got two chairs from the corner of the room and put them in front of John and Mary. "I really don't want to do this, but it's the only way."

The three men got off John's back and lifted his frail body. He tried to fight, but they quickly forced him into the chair. Thaddaeus pressed his giant hands down on his shoulders to keep him from getting up as Phillip removed his belt and started tying one of John's legs to the chair legs.

"Are you really going to tie us up?" John asked in shock. "Look at all we have been through the last three years. Does that mean nothing to you?"

"I could say the same thing to you, John," Peter spoke up. "Look at all we have been through the last three years, and you weren't going to side with us." He stepped away and looked out the window, hearing the quiet of the city. "If you are not for us, you are against us."

"Peter," John said discouragingly, "I was only trying to save you all. That's all we were going to do. We weren't going to come and attack you to keep you from doing what you are planning to do."

"If there were more of you," Peter started as he watched intently from the window, "I bet you would have done the same thing."

"We would have never tied you up, Peter," Mary said through a sniffling nose. "We would have never treated you like this."

Chapter 60
Mary Magdalene

"We would have never treated you like this," I said as Andrew started to tie my feet to the chair legs.

"For some reason, I have a hard time believing that," Peter said unconvincingly. "I have a really hard time."

I looked over at John who was being tied up like a common animal, as if binding him for torture or a sacrifice. I couldn't believe my blurry eyes. I was hoping I wasn't seeing correctly. Oh, how I prayed this was just a delusion and the tear drops were reflecting an incorrect image in my eyes. But as I tried to wiggle my left leg, I knew my eyes were not deceiving me. I was being tied down as well.

"We need more straps," Andrew said as they had used multiple belts and sashes on each of John's legs and even tied his hands together behind his back.

"Want to blindfold me too?" John asked sarcastically as he rolled his eyes.

I almost grinned at his comment. John had grown so much in the last year. He wasn't the same young boy as when I first met him. He was still a gawky teenager, growing taller and thinner each day, but he was maturing. He still had a baby face any mother would love, but his eyes had a look of wisdom many men three times his age lacked.

They couldn't find any more strips of cloth, so I spoke up. "I'm not going to go anywhere. You don't have to tie me any further."

Peter huffed at the comment. "Thanks, Mary, but I think we will just play it safe," he said as he grabbed a knife from his sack and started cutting away strips of cloth from the hem of his robe. "I think we will have plenty," he said looking up at me as he continued to cut a few more strips. "But thanks for your concern."

"Peter," I said trying to talk reasonably with him as he focused on cutting his robe. "Peter, look at me." But still he didn't look up. It was as if he was ignoring me because I knew he clearly heard me. I even saw his eyes roll as I said his name the first time. "Peter!"

"What!" he snapped. "What do you want to say, Mary? What is so important?"

I just shook my head and thought back to all the times we had spent together in the last year. Listening to Jesus teach, seeing him perform wonders and signs no one else would even dare to try, watching him show love and respect to everyone he met. Jesus never acted like this. I wanted to start shaking my fist at him, but I knew it was useless. He wouldn't listen. Even if I performed a miracle just like Jesus, he would turn a blind eye to the amazement.

"Pharisee," I muttered under my breath. I witnessed the looks Peter was giving me, and they looked just like the blank, uncompassionate stares the council gave Jesus all the time. Even as he spoke of logic and reason, they couldn't hear it. Even as Jesus spoke of love and forgiveness, they wouldn't stand for it. Even as Jesus spoke of correction and repentance at their erroneous ways, they couldn't see they were in the wrong.

In their eyes they were blameless. They were above the law. They were always right.

Peter was turning into them.

"Here," Peter said to Thomas giving him some of the strips. "Tie her down and gag her so she won't disturb us anymore."

"Gag her?"

Chapter 61
Thomas

"Gag her?" I said with a quivering voice. "I don't think we have to do that, Peter," I said feebly.

"If you don't do it, I will," Peter said forcefully as he looked at a few of the others. "Let's get back to what you were saying."

They started telling more of the details they had discovered throughout the day. A few of them gave their ideas of the best places to attack the guards, but I stopped listening. All I could hear was the pounding of my heart in my chest, deafening my sense of hearing from everything else.

"I'm sor..." I started to say to Mary, but she didn't even look at me as I tied her free leg to the chair. I wanted her to look at me, but she wouldn't. And I didn't blame her. I tenderly grabbed her hands, gently pulling them behind her back. I carefully tied them together, trying to not cause her any pain. The emotional pain was enough for her to take.

I stood up and wrapped the last strip around her head, placing the fabric in her mouth. She looked defeated. I felt deflated. We were both losing ourselves in this upper room.

I looked at the table where the rest of the men were huddled around, remembering how we were clinging onto one another last night. I had squeezed tightly the hands that were nearby because I was afraid of what the next day was going to hold. I wondered if any of us realized we should have been frightened by our own thoughts that ran rampant through the darkness. I looked at John and Mary, tied like enemy captives and got a sickening memory of one of Jesus' teachings when he'd recited the scriptures from Solomon.

"My son," he had said compassionately and enthusiastically one evening as we were falling asleep under the canvas of stars overhead, "do not forget my teaching, but let your heart keep my commandments, for length of days and years of life and peace they will add to you."

He had stood up and looked around at anyone who was still awake and I sat up as well to let him know I was still listening. "Let not steadfast love and faithfulness forsake you; but bind them around your neck; write them on the tablet of your heart. So you will find favor and good success in the sight of God and man."

He had smiled at me, and slowly a few others rose from their pillows made of leaves and dirt. "Trust in the Lord with all your heart, and do not lean on your own understanding. In all your ways acknowledge him, and he will make straight your paths. Be not wise in your own eyes; fear the Lord, and turn away from evil."

Then he had stopped saying the words of King Solomon and started blessing each of us, asking us to always trust in the Lord and not to lean on ourselves for understanding. "When you start to lean on yourself, you will eventually fall."

I closed my eyes in regret at what I had just done. I had turned my back on my two friends. Instead of binding my friend with love and faithfulness, I gagged her with silent fear.

I hoped they would soon understand me. Understand my motives.

I turned to walk away and felt my legs trip at a raised board in the floor. I tried to stop myself from falling, but I couldn't.

I heard Mary mumble something, but I knew what she said. Even though it wasn't clear, her eyes spoke the words she was saying. She was the only one in the room to ask if I was okay.

I nodded my head and stood up. I walked over to the window and saw a Roman guard walk by. I didn't look at him with hatred. I didn't look at him with contempt. A rare emotion for the Roman guard rose up in my heart, bubbling until it felt like it was crawling on my skin.

I felt sorry for him. Even though they had treated us cruelly, he was just doing his job. I looked back and saw Mary and John tied up.

I was just as bad as the Roman guard. I was just doing a job someone told me to do. Just like them, I didn't speak up. I was just as bad. Or maybe I was worse, because I did know better. I knew what Jesus said to me over the last three years. I still remembered many of those cherished moments when he would walk beside me and speak encouragement into my heart. He never told me I couldn't do it. He'd always said I could.

"Thomas, get away from that window," Peter barked. I ignored his comment. I was tired of listening to people I wasn't sure I should trust. But sadly, I wondered if I would feel the same way in a few hours.

Would I act just like a Roman soldier again?

"What happened here?"

Chapter 62

James

"What happened here?" I asked breathlessly after running up the stairs with all the information I had obtained from hiding outside of the Roman guard's house. "John!" I exclaimed before turning to see the other person. "Mary!"

"Leave them," Peter commanded from the table as the majority of the men were huddled around him. "What do you have?"

I looked at John who didn't even make a sound. My heart broke as I saw Mary raise her head and saw her mouth was covered with a piece of fabric to keep her from talking. "Why are they tied up?" I asked confused, bending over my brother to untie his legs.

"I wouldn't do that unless you want to be tied up too," John whispered into my ear.

"We didn't hurt them," Andrew said, pushing me away from John and moving me closer to the table to sit and discuss all my new knowledge.

I felt like I was floating as I was being escorted to the table, leaving my beloved brother bound to a chair. It was like he was being made into an example of his defiance for anyone else who might question the motives for tonight.

I was torn between the two. I wanted to be with my brother and untie the knots, but I also wanted to support my new brothers and help with their goal. I started telling them all the information on the Roman guard and wondered which was right.

Is doing nothing or something the right choice for now?

I didn't know the answer. Last night, I thought every one was on board except for Mary since she left before we started seriously talking of Peter's revolutionary plan. I knew John was silent through most of the night, but silence didn't always mean opposition. Silence was sometimes reserved support.

"James, we don't have a lot of time," Peter once again said from the planning table. "We need to know what you have found out."

I started telling everyone in the room what I had discovered during my day of lurking outside the guard's home and stalking his movements, which were few and far between.

I looked over at John who seemed like a hundred miles away. He stared at the ceiling as I spoke as if trying to ignore the discussion a few cubits away.

"He's going to be on duty tonight from dusk to dawn," I said, watching my little brother safely from the chasm between us. I wanted him to know even though I was on this side of the room, I was still his brother.

"Where?" several of the others started asking at once.

"He's going to be guarding the tomb," I said solemnly. I didn't know why saying the words caused a well of emotions inside me, but it did. Maybe it was the fact everything was swirling together faster than I had anticipated. Maybe it was that a few days ago we were united, but now our group had split in various ways. Jesus was killed. Judas killed himself. Mary and John were bound.

It seemed like everything Jesus had been building over the last three years had quickly started crumbling in just two days. Thoughts of trust and brotherhood were dashed with questions of loyalty. People I believed were sturdy and strong, deeply rooted and tethered together a few days ago, were the ones swept under the tidal wave first.

I couldn't help myself, but the words escaped my lips faster than I could hold them back. I saw the look in Peter's eyes as I voiced my concerns.

"What if this isn't right?"

Peter's plan was to surprise attack the first guard. The guard would be standing before my friend's tomb. It sickened me to think the first time I would be going to Jesus' tomb wouldn't be out of condolences on his death. No, it would be to strike revenge. We were going to kill a man in front of the tomb of a man who condemned murder. We were plotting to avenge the innocent death of Jesus when Jesus never spoke a word of retaliation. He urged the opposite.

"Temptations to sin are sure to come," Jesus had said one day as he was teaching to us. "But woe to the one through who they come!" he'd cried out, almost in pain, as if the sins we would commit hurt him in some way.

He had looked around and found a heavy rock on the ground. "It would be better for him if a millstone were hung around his neck and he were cast into the sea than that he should cause one of these little ones to sin." He'd walked around and placed his hands on each of us. We were his little ones. Peter was the oldest, but he was still significantly younger than Jesus, in his early twenties.

"Pay attention to yourselves! If your brother sins, rebuke him, and if he repents, forgive him, and if he sins against you seven times in the day, and turns to you seven times saying, 'I repent,' you must forgive him," Jesus had said as he concluded his message.

I looked around the room now and my insides were churning. I couldn't help myself, but the questions were mounting heavier than a millstone around my neck. I looked out the window and started to see the darkness of night creep into our room. Another day had gone.

The Sabbath was almost over. There was no way I could say I kept this day holy. Not today.

"You're not doubting, are you?" Peter asked, looking at me with contempt. My eyes darted to the others around the table, and even though they didn't speak, their eyes asked the same question.

I didn't answer, because I was doubting everything.

"We need you, James," Peter said walking over to me and placing his hands on my shoulder. I didn't feel comforted. I felt bullied.

I looked at him and nodded my head. *Temptations to sin are sure to come,* echoed in my head, as if Jesus was standing beside me whispering the delicate words. It was a haunting sound, but I didn't know what scared me the most – the memory of his voice or my lack of obedience.

"You all get some rest," Peter said as he looked around the room. "We are going to need to be at our best to accomplish this tonight."

They agreed and found a few pillows and mats in the corner and formed makeshift beds.

I couldn't sleep. My thoughts were scattered, and peace seemed unattainable. I looked out the window and saw a Roman guard walking down the road. I watched overhead as he passed by and noticed he didn't look like a killer. He stood tall, shoulders back, hand on the tang of his sword in case he needed to use it.

He never said a word.

He just calmly whistled.

Chapter 63

Atticus – Roman Guard

The city was eerily quiet and calm this Saturday night, but most Saturday nights were due to the Jewish holy day. But something was different. I started to whistle to end the silence. The streets were empty. Even the homes were quiet as I made my way to the tomb of the Jewish leader that was executed yesterday.

I expected to see something, but it appeared the overcast sky caused everyone to stay indoors. It looked like it was going to storm once again and I desperately wished it wouldn't rain through the night. There was nothing worse than standing in the rain for hours on end – except maybe standing guard for no reason than to keep the peace in the Jewish community.

Walking the lonely streets and alleys of Jerusalem always caused me to keep my hand on the grip of my sword. I had seen too many soldiers in my time that were not prepared and died or were seriously injured because that second to find their sword was a second too long. I promised myself I wasn't going to be naïve to believe the Jews would never rise up against us. My wife heard the whispers in the market that would suddenly hush when she would walk up.

I never heard the whispers.

I only heard their shouts. Very rarely did they follow through on the threats, but I was always prepared. Always.

I looked up the lonely road and saw a garden near the tomb that was just a hole cut into a rock with a large boulder in front as protection from vandals or scavengers.

"Atticus," one of the guards said as I approached.

"Titus," I returned. "Anything that I need to be aware of?"

Titus looked over at Felix as they both shook their heads. "Just an occasional bird," Titus answered undisturbed. "That was about it."

"Great, so, it's going to be a long, pointless night," I said agitated.

"It could be worse," Felix commented as he noticed the other guard was heading our way. "It looks like rain for you," he chuckled at my expense.

"I was thinking the same thing," I huffed feeling a few sprinkles.

"Who's that coming?" he asked.

"Oh, that's Longinus," I answered squinting my eyes to see. "At least it's supposed to be him." I watched as he slowly made his way to the tomb, taking his time and enjoying the dusky atmosphere. "Why do we have to have two people guarding the tomb? Seems unnecessary to me. We could have worked this shift alone."

"Enjoy the company," Titus remarked. "It's going to be a long, boring night. How are you, Longinus?" he asked as the approaching soldier kicked a few rocks walking the last bit of the path to the tomb.

"I'm doing," Longinus answered distracted. "I'm just doing."

Chapter 64

Longinus

"I'm just doing," I said feeling uneasy now standing in front of the tomb of the man I didn't know, yet wanted to know more about. Not much had changed in the last twenty-four hours from when I was at this man's tomb before.

I still felt a heaviness. I couldn't shake it. I spoke to my wife and she thought I was losing my mind. "Maybe you need to ask for a reassignment," she had said as she reclined beside me this afternoon.

I didn't think a reassignment would fix my attitude on this, because truthfully, I didn't know what my problem was. I didn't have any rational explanation why I was feeling like this, except when I stood under the man on the cross after I pierced his side I felt something different. He wasn't a common criminal like the other two.

I considered going to the synagogue today to ask some questions, but I didn't think it would do any good because the crowd roared for him to be crucified yesterday. They wouldn't say anything positive. It was as if his massive following dissipated in the blink of an eye.

But I knew he still had some followers out there.

I just had to find them.

I didn't know who I was going to be looking for. And if I asked around for his followers, they would probably deny it. I looked like a Roman and they would probably think it was a trick to capture them as well. I was caught in a difficult position, wanting to know more about him and unable to understand how I could learn more.

"Have a good evening," Titus and Felix commented as they left quickly, running as the raindrops grew from sprinkles to buckets.

"This is just great," Atticus said with disdain looking around the area for a place to hide from the pelting rain while still guarding the dead man's tomb. "Stay here," he said jogging off into the nearby garden.

I turned my body and touched the stone standing at the entrance of his tomb. The rain was causing the grayish boulder to look slick and clean. It was a surreal thought that death was behind the wall placed here. On one side was life and reality, and on the other was death and the unknown.

I wondered, *Why do I really care about this man I never met before? Why am I wasting all this time considering when I don't even know if he is legitimate?*

I turned around and saw Atticus running towards me. "We can sit up on the hill and watch the tomb under the tree."

"Do you think it will be okay?" I asked, wondering if our commander, Maximus, would say it was all right.

"I could see you perfectly clear from up there," he answered. "It should be fine, but let's leave a torch down here so we can see it through the night." He started to laugh, "Because so many people are probably going to come by here to steal the body."

I nodded my head as he continued.

"Even if they do come to take the body, that huge stone will take a few strong men to move. By time they start moving it, we will be down here and subdue their scheme," he said authoritatively.

We walked to the garden and he was right. I could see everything happening at the tomb from under the protection of the tree limbs. Yet, I still felt vulnerable.

We stood on guard from the garden, keeping watch over the tomb. We still did our shift as we were trained, just thirty cubits away.

I looked down at the lonely tomb. I wondered what his friends and family were doing at this moment since they were not allowed to come to the tomb on their holy day. Were they celebrating this man's life? Were they wallowing in sadness from his untimely death? Were they together or suffering alone?

Questions continued to rise, and the unknown answers nagged me.

"Weird weather we've been having," Atticus commented as he looked up at the nighttime sky. "An earthquake and a second day of storms."

"Mm-hmm," I agreed.

"Have you even been in an earthquake before yesterday?" he asked. Usually Atticus wasn't into small talk, but just as Felix and Titus noted, it was going to be a long night.

I shook my head no.

"You okay?" he asked.

I knew we didn't have a strong emotional tie binding us together. We were just soldiers under the same command. If we didn't work together, we wouldn't have anything else in common, most likely.

My ears perked as I heard something faintly in the distance.

"Shhh," I whispered. "Do you hear that?"

He shook his head no, but I could tell he was leaning his ear into the distance, straining to catch what I was hearing. And I actually did hear something. It wasn't just deflecting his question.

"Where?"

Chapter 65

James

"Where?" I asked Peter and Thaddaeus who came with me. "Where is the guard?"

I couldn't see their faces, but I saw them look at one another, as if asking themselves if they believed me.

"I heard him say he was going to be here tonight," I said in shock. "I heard him telling his wife the priest requested guards at the tomb and he got this shift," I quickly defended. "I promise." I knew what I heard.

"They might have changed plans," Peter said agitatedly. "It's not your fault," he said shaking his head. "You wouldn't have known."

Peter stopped walking up to the tomb and started to turn around as I continued.

"Let's go back," Peter commanded.

"Give me a minute," I said walking further up the path until I was a few cubits from the tomb, brightly lit with fiery torches on each side. I hadn't been to the tomb to pay my respects. I had stayed hidden yesterday and today.

"Jesus," I moaned softly as I felt the hard, wet cold stone. I wanted to place my ear to the rock and pretend Jesus wasn't dead but sleeping. That if I stood there long enough I could hear a faint snoring sound.

The only sound I heard was the rain hitting the ground, splashing in the puddles left from yesterday's storm. I laid my head against the rock and something caught my attention in the garden, a withered tree.

It reminded me of a tree Jesus had cursed somewhere outside the city limits.

We had been coming from Bethany when Jesus noticed a bare tree with only leaves. "May no one ever eat fruit from you again," he'd said which confused me. *Why say something like that to a tree?*

The next day we came by the same fig tree and it was dead. One day it was alive with green leaves and strong roots deep in the ground, and the next day it looked like it just gave up and died.

Peter had turned to Jesus and pointed out the tree.

"Have faith in God," Jesus said and then took a moment to teach. "Truly, I say to you, whoever says to this mountain, 'Be taken up and thrown into the sea,' and does not doubt in his heart, but believes that what he says will come to pass, it will be done for him. Therefore I tell you, whatever you ask in prayer, believe that you have received it, and it will be yours. And whenever you stand praying, forgive, if you have anything against anyone, so that your Father also who is in heaven may forgive you your trespasses."

Now I turned my attention from the tree in the garden and stared at the rock before me.

"Jesus! Rise!" I yelled.

I stood back expecting something to happen, but I couldn't tell if my prayer had been answered. I found the edge of the rock where it sealed the tomb and tried to force a finger in the space to see if I could hear anything. "Come on, Jesus! Breathe and come out!"

I tried to grip the stone and move it out of the way, but it was too slippery from the sudden downpour. My fingers couldn't find any

227

broken or rough part of the rock to hold onto and try to open the tomb.

"Please, Jesus! Please!" I moaned. I put my ear to the crevasse but couldn't hear anything. It hadn't budged enough for a grain of sand to slip through.

I continued to push the rock as I heard shouts from behind.

"Stop!" two men yelled from the distance. It didn't sound like Peter or Thaddaeus, but I didn't know who else it could be. We were all alone.

I didn't stop. I thought I misheard their voices and they would come up beside me to help move the stone.

"I said stop!" one of the voices said again. This time I knew it wasn't anyone I knew and the dialect in his tone wasn't Jewish. I knew in my gut who the men were now running towards me as I heard their feet stomping through the sloshing mud, coming closer and closer.

I thought about turning around and facing the guards like a man.

But then I had another thought.

Run.

My instincts kicked in and I ran behind the tomb in the opposite direction of where Peter and Thaddaeus were standing. I realized with each stride I didn't have the ambition to kill anyone.

I was too scared.

I didn't look back. I thought if I kept running the guards would eventually stop and return to their post. I kept running until I got to the city walls, but I still didn't feel like stopping. I knew inside the city walls was a safer place to be than outside them, but right then, I didn't feel safe anywhere.

I snuck through a hole in the wall the townspeople used when they wanted to enter and leave undetected. I slipped through the hole and started running again. The wetness on my face was no longer just rain, but sweat and tears as well.

My legs started to give out. My lungs were screaming in pain from the sudden burst of energy. I let my body tumble onto the path as a bed of mud softened my fall. I took in a few deep breaths as the rain continued to fall on my back. I wanted to lie in the mud forever. I wanted to pretend like nothing was wrong. I wanted to forget about the plan for revenge. I wanted to ignore the fact Jesus was dead. Even though I had learned so much in the last three years, I now wished those three years never existed.

I just wanted the memory of how things were to be blotted from my memory. I wanted a clean slab to make new memories, or to try to make a new life without the effects of the last two days.

I knew I was asking for too much. I rolled off my stomach and off the path dragging my body next to a tree. I wanted to rest against something that would give me some type of support.

I leaned against the trunk, but I didn't feel the strength I desperately needed. I felt my body weight cracking the sturdy tree. I traced my fingers on the ground and found a few of the roots protruding; they were not strong and intact, but loose and fragile. I glanced up as lightning struck in the distance and I saw the empty branches. There was no life in the tree. No leaves clinging to the branches. It looked like a pair of old, dead hands spreading its fingers to the heavens.

And whenever you stand praying, I heard Jesus' voice say from a memory, *forgive, if you have anything against anyone, so that your Father also who is in heaven may forgive you your trespasses.*

I started to cry as lightning struck again in the distance. I had found myself at another dead tree.

The tree Jesus cursed a few days ago.

"Are you all right?"

Chapter 66
Nicodemus

"Are you all right?" I asked the crying young man huddled under the withered tree. "Let me help you up."

"I'm okay," the young man said, lying through his teeth.

"You're covered in mud, it's raining, and it's late," I persuaded. "Please, let me take you home and get you cleaned up."

He didn't reject my offer. He stood up and tried to rake off as much mud as he could from the front of his robe. He glanced up at me looking as if he had been disgraced.

"It is okay," I said warmly. "We have all been at the bottom a time or two."

He nodded his head and agreed as we started to walk.

"My name is Nicodemus," I said, trying to see his profile in the dark.

"James," he said timidly.

"Are you from around here, because you look slightly familiar," I said as my aged eyes started to focus in the darkness. He had a way about him I believed I had seen before, but being a rabbi, I saw a lot of people.

"No, I'm from Gennesaret," he said softly.

"You look like a fisherman," I said with a smile as we were approaching the entrance.

"I used to be," he said and then corrected, "or I am, or I will be again soon," he said with a hint of uncertainty. "It's been a confusing week."

"Mm-hmm. That is indeed an understatement," I said thinking back on the last few days.

We walked in silence through the deserted streets of Jerusalem. I grabbed a torch lying on the ground and lit it from one of the few torches along the road. I looked over at him and his face still looked very familiar. Then I started to figure it out.

"So, you came here for Passover?" I asked, looking down and seeing his muddy robe had been slightly cleansed by the rain shower.

"Yes," he said.

"How was your Passover?" I asked, but he didn't answer. He just shook his head and closed his eyes, as if remembering the torrid events that had transpired in the last few days.

"Did you know the man that was crucified?" I asked. "His name was Jesus of Nazareth."

I could tell I might have upset him because he didn't respond. His breathing stopped. I looked over and saw his eyes darting around trying to find a place to run off to. I knew I needed to ease his mind.

"He was a good man," I said looking straight ahead at the path. "A very wise and good man."

"What makes you say that?" he asked.

I wondered if he was afraid I was trying to trap him. I needed to give him some security. "I have watched him for some time," I said with a smile. "He was much, much younger than I, but he had a way with his words. I do have to admit sometimes when he spoke, I didn't understand him, but he was always patient to explain the deeper meaning. Sometime I got it and other times I walked away with more questions."

232

He nodded as I spoke as if we were on the same level.

"He didn't deserve what happened to him," I said in a tone of condolence. "Mary didn't deserve to see..." I started to say as he stopped me.

"You know Mary?" he asked with a heightened tone of amazement.

"I do," I said with a nod. "I was with her as we buried him yesterday." I shook my head in sadness. "He didn't deserve this."

"I was..." he started to say but then stopped to look around to see if it was safe. "I was one of..." he once again started but then stopped as if fear caught ahold of his words.

I could hear the heaviness in his voice. He wanted to say the words, but didn't have the boldness to utter a simple sentence. So, I finished it for him. "I know, James," I said turning down an alley. "My home is just a little ways ahead."

"How'd you know?"

I didn't know exactly how I knew, but it all fit. "Because I feel just like you do, son," I started. "You may have the mud on your robe, but I have the mud on my heart." We walked a little ways in silence. I kept the torch lifted high to let him see his surroundings. I didn't want him to think I was leading him on a deathly journey of regret and imprisonment. "We are in the same boat, my son."

"But you're a..." he started to say. I knew he was referring to my rabbi garments.

"Even rabbis search for answers," I said stopping in front of my darkened home and opening the door to let him in. "It sickens me to think my friends of many years could have done such a thing. To act

233

on their fear and anger to kill an innocent man." I started lighting a few candles to welcome him. I let him wait by the door as I got a basin of water and a fresh robe to change into.

He listened to my words as I spoke. I started to wipe down his hands and feet of the watery mud that encased them. He took off his outer robe as I stepped away to allow him privacy to clean himself and put on the clean robe. When I returned he had a different way about him. He wasn't the same young man as when I found him. He had a look in his eyes resembling one with a mission to fulfill.

He gave me back the basin of murky water and thanked me for my kindness.

I smiled. "You can stay here for the night," I said dumping the basin outside my front door. "But I feel like you probably have somewhere else you need to go."

His eyes lit up.

"Am I right?"

He nodded his head and thanked me for my hospitality.

"Before you go, do you want a bite to eat?" I asked. "At least stay until the storm lets up. I would hate for you to get my robe filthy," I said with a lighthearted laugh. "Old rags are hard to keep looking new."

He obliged and broke bread with me. It was comforting to sit with someone else this dreary night. I had wrestled with myself too much last night wondering what I could have done to stop what had happened. I wrestled with myself so much I could barely move. Jacob got off easy with just a wounded hip. I had a wounded heart.

I looked outside the window as we finished our meal and noticed the rain was easing up. The heavy downpour seemed to have settled into a drizzle.

"Seems like now may be the best time to go," I said taking his empty plate. "But I'm not forcing you to leave."

"No, I understand," he said rising from the table. "But it's time."

Chapter 67

James

"But it's time," I said thanking Nicodemus for everything he had done for me this evening. "You may never know how much you helped tonight."

He eyed me encouragingly, "I think I will learn one day."

I waved goodbye as he stood at the door, offering me a torch. I considered taking it, but I declined. I didn't want to be seen where I was going.

The rain had diminished, but it wasn't totally finished. I left the warm, security of Nicodemus' home and headed out in the uncertain. I knew where my destination was going to lead me, but I hadn't come up with anything after that. I hoped I had a few hours to contemplate, pray, and decide the best move to make.

The streets were quiet, just as they had been when we walked to the tomb earlier. Although earlier I had been walking with a team, whereas now, I was an army of one. But I knew ultimately, I wasn't alone. I had a team waiting for me.

I looked up at the sky and noticed a lone star shining overhead. Clouds continued to swirl, swiftly moving across the midnight sky, but they seemed to always miss that beam of light. It was like the star was leading me on a journey and letting me know I was going to be safe.

I remembered the various times I had felt scared in the last three years. I was amazed at how Jesus exuded love and compassion, yet so many people hated and despised him. One evening after he had eluded a mass stoning from the Pharisees, a few of us had asked if he was scared.

He just shook his head and said, "The Lord is my shepherd; I shall not want. He makes me lie down in green pasture. He leads me beside still waters. He restores my soul. He leads me in paths of righteousness for his name's sake." He stopped and looked at each of us and smiled.

He then began again, "Even though I walk through the valley of the shadow of death, I will fear no evil, for you are with me; your rod and your staff, they comfort me. You prepare a table before me in the presence of my enemies; you anoint my head with oil; my cup overflows."

He took a moment and looked up at the heavens, lifting his hands to the sky. "Surely goodness and mercy will follow me all the days of my life, and I shall dwell in the house of the Lord forever."

He stopped speaking and once again answered our question. "See why I'm not scared. God the Father tells us to not be scared. He is always there to comfort us when we need comforting."

I turned down another alley and made my way to my destination. I started saying the same words with an earnest plea for some comfort. As I spoke, I felt a wave wash over me. As if I was anointed.

I was being comforted.

I continued to say the words over and over, looking up at my closest friend on this walk. The star still hadn't left me.

I turned one last time and saw the home I was heading toward. I didn't want to go in but preferred to wait outside in the darkness, where no one would know I was around. I found a few crates and barrels and created a barrier where I could see others but hopefully remain hidden. I positioned myself directly under the window. Suddenly, my friend disappeared. It was as if it had stayed beside me during the trek, leading me to where I needed to go.

I tucked my knees into my chest and closed my eyes although I knew sleep wasn't permitted.

As my eyes closed, my other senses intensified and took its place. I could smell the musty aroma of the puddled rain water. I could feel a light sprinkle tapping ever so gently on the crown of my head. And I could faintly hear the sound of multiple people snoring.

I waited. I didn't want to hear their blissful sleep. I wanted to hear something else.

Suddenly, I heard a mumbled whisper. I couldn't make out the words, so I focused even more on the sound. I longed to hear pronunciations and not slurred speech. Suddenly, it happened.

"When do you want to wake them?"

Chapter 68
Thaddaeus

"When do you want to wake them?" I asked Peter as all the men were lying on the floor, resting like we should have been. But I didn't want to leave Peter awake. I could tell he wouldn't be sleeping, even though I had mentioned to him multiple times he needed to get some rest. Maybe it would clear his mind, but he had gotten angry with my suggestion.

He'd snapped at me. "Why do you think I need to clear my mind? Are you having second thoughts?"

"No, no, no," I had tried to reassure him, but his body language proved I hadn't done so. He just looked annoyed that I was sitting beside him with my droopy eyes begging for a little rest. I rested my head on the table but didn't fall asleep.

"We can give them a little more time, but then we will have to go out and start this, this…" he stopped and looked at me. "I don't know what to call what we are doing."

I shrugged my shoulders and couldn't think of the word he wanted either.

He started flinching and shaking his fist. "What is wrong with me? I can't even think of a simple word!"

I didn't know how to respond. I had my opinion, but I had already given it multiple times and it hadn't done any good so far. So I just remained silent and laid my head down on the table again.

"Don't worry about it," I said. "It doesn't matter what it's called."

"Yeah, but I just feel like my mind is spinning out of control," he said standing up to pace in front of the open window. "Right when I think of something, I lose it and then something else comes up. It's like I'm chasing a fleeting thought and then I can't even remember what I'm chasing in the first place. Does that make sense?"

"Um…"

"Am I losing it?" he asked looking squarely into my eyes. I knew what I wanted to say, but I didn't know what I would actually say.

Chapter 69

Peter

"Am I losing it?" I asked Thaddaeus. By his lack of words, he knew I was. He looked at me like I was losing my last grip of reality.

"I told you my opinion earlier and you didn't want to hear it, but I think you just need to take a break," he said sympathetically. "You have been going nonstop on this manic mission for the last two days, and now it is catching up with you. The rage is tiring you out."

"*My* rage?" I asked bewildered. "It's not just my rage, but all of ours."

"Let's be fair," he said softly. "You were the one who came up with the plan. Before you, we were just scared men wondering what we were going to do next."

"So, I'm confused," I said shaking my head to make some sense of the words he uttered. "Are you going to go with me or not, Thaddaeus?"

"Peter, you need to rest," he said without answering the question.

"But I need to stay awake," I said, recalling a memory from two nights ago.

"Sit here, while I go over there and pray," Jesus had said to me, James, and John in the Garden of Gethsemane. He had looked deeply troubled and I started to pray, but something happened.

Next thing I knew, Jesus had returned. "So, could you not watch with me one hour? Watch and pray that you may not enter into temptation. The spirit indeed is willing, but the flesh is weak."

I couldn't believe how badly I had let Jesus down and started praying like he asked. But once again, something happened.

"Sleep and take your rest later on," Jesus had said returning. Once again I had failed him. I'd tried to apologize, but all I could get out was a yawn. I had looked over at James and John who also had fallen asleep. I saw the look of shame on their faces and knew mine reflected theirs.

"See, the hour is at hand, and the Son of Man is betrayed into the hands of sinners. Rise, let us be going, see, my betrayer is at hand."

The three of us had slowly stood and stretched our bodies starting to question what Jesus had just said when we saw Judas Iscariot coming toward us. I wondered why Judas Iscariot was coming with the betrayer. Even in that moment, I still couldn't see Judas as the betrayer. I didn't know if I was too tired to see the truth or if I didn't want to believe it.

All I knew was I had failed Jesus when I fell asleep those two times. I wasn't going to fail him again while avenging his murder.

"The spirit is willing, but the flesh is weak, Thaddaeus," I said to him as he lifted his head and looked at me in confusion.

"What does that mean?"

"It means we have to do this. We can't give up," I said. "We need to pray."

"Okay," he said with an unsure tone.

"Please, when Jesus faced hard times, he always went and prayed," I urged. "So we need to pray."

I heard Thaddaeus start to pray. I went over and knelt in the corner to focus my attention solely on the upcoming plan.

I heard the sounds in the room, and the snoring soothed my aching soul. I listened to the breathing patterns like they were waves on the sea that always caused me to sleep so well. Thaddaeus' murmuring quieted until it finally ended.

I didn't look up but assumed he fell asleep. I shook my head annoyed, realizing how Jesus must have felt with me. My heart sank at how disloyal I had been to him in his final moment of need. I thought back at how earnestly I had been praying, but I couldn't help myself; I kept falling asleep as I prayed, even though I knew how important it was to him.

I kept thinking of that crucial moment in the garden of Gethsemane. How I had raised the white flag at the battle but had fallen victim to my flesh. I lost my focus on the mission two nights ago.

Just as I did just now.

A familiar feeling came over me.

I fell asleep.

THE NEXT DAY

Chapter 70
Peter

I awoke in the corner, still lying down in a curled up position. My heart stopped at how I had messed up so badly. I glanced around the darkened room and commanded everyone to wake up. I didn't know how long I had been asleep. I could have been out five minutes or five hours, but luckily the sun hadn't risen yet.

The guard was still at the tomb.

"Come on! Come on!" I billowed, stomping around the room waking everyone up. "We have to move, people!"

Thaddaeus shot up as if found guilty of a crime. He had fallen asleep too. "I'm sorry," he stammered as he groggily stood up, moving around the room as if he had drunk too much wine the night before, even though I knew he hadn't. His mind still hadn't fully woken up.

I looked over and saw John and Mary still tied up. I started to feel horrible about the way I was treating them. Mary opened her eyes and looked around the room. John's eyes were wide awake at the commotion and quickly checked on Mary.

"Mary, how are you holding up?" he asked looking at her and then staring menacingly at me. "Do you need something to drink or eat?"

She nodded her head yes. My remorse was growing; even as John was tied up, he was still looking out for someone else.

"Can someone get her something to drink?" John asked as I walked over to the basin and dipped her a cup.

I removed the strips of cloth and noticed they were laced with dirt from the hem of my robe. She never complained when we gagged her with dirty fabric. She didn't holler or fuss throughout the night. She remained calm and cordial watching our every move throughout the night.

"Here, Mary," I said kindly. "Drink."

She looked up at me with tired and emotionally fueled eyes. She took in as much water as her mouth could hold. I thought she was going to spit it back into my face, since that was something I would probably consider. But she didn't.

She swallowed the refreshing water and then opened her mouth again to have the gag placed into her mouth.

"Mary, you know I'm not like this," I said defensively, stooping down to my knees so our eyes were on an equal level. "You know, don't you?"

She thought for a few seconds and then spoke. "Yes, I know you are not like this. That is why I think you are making a big mistake."

I let her speak, but I wasn't ready to hear it. I stood up and walked back to the basin to put up the cup as she continued to pull at my heart.

But she didn't know my heart was broken. And I didn't know if it would ever get fixed.

The rest of the group started stirring around the room as I took control of the situation.

"James, Matthew, Phillip, and Bartholomew, I want you to go in pairs; two of you go to the front entrance gates and two of you go to the Roman command post," I said looking down at our notes we had taken yesterday evening. "Thaddaeus," I stopped and looked around the room, "where's the other James?"

"He never returned last night," John spoke from his bound chair.

"We will have to go on without him. Thaddaeus, I want you to find a hiding spot along the path from the tomb to the command post. That way, in case a guard finds out what we did, you can stop the guard."

"Stop the guard?" Thaddaeus asked hesitantly. "Do you mean stop or do you mean…" but he couldn't finish the question.

"I think you know what I mean," I said unemotionally as I had a mission to fulfill. "Kill. Do you have a problem with that?"

"I just thought…" Thaddaeus started to say, but then stopped as he saw Peter's unfriendly gaze. "Message received," he said, nodding and slinking back against the wall.

"Andrew and Thomas, you will go with me to the tomb. And Simon, you will stay and watch over John and Mary."

"Why does Simon get to stay?" Andrew asked.

"Would you rather stay back here and watch over them, little brother?" I asked sinisterly. "Stay back and do nothing as the others are out risking their lives? I thought you were better than that, Andrew."

Andrew quickly shook his head and apologized.

"Does anyone want to back out?" I asked, looking around the room. They didn't look like a strong set of soldiers compared to the Roman forces, but they would have to do. No one said anything. No one stepped up and said they wanted to stay back.

No one.

"This is not going to be an easy task, but I believe we can do it," I started with conviction. "This soldier we are going after killed Jesus.

He will be the first sacrifice we make and then there will be others. This may be a long day, but it will be worth it. I am sorry to say, but look around this room. The people standing here now may not be standing here tonight. Once we kill the first and they find out, we will have to stand our ground. Do not be foolish. If there is a soldier by himself, get him yourself. If there is someone nearby watching, do not do anything. They could scream and then other people may be around. We want to do this methodically and carefully. This is not going to be an easy doing. And we may all die, but at least we will have tried."

"Please, don't do this."

Chapter 71

Mary Magdalene

"Please, don't do this," I pleaded. I didn't want to be gagged again, but I didn't want my friends and brothers to go off to a losing war. "You are all going to die," I warned with tears starting to stream down my face. "Look around the room," I said with heartfelt agony. "If it starts today, you will not return. You are just young men who have never done anything like this. The Roman guards have trained their entire lives. You are making a grave mistake."

I looked around the room and saw the young faces looking at me. They were faces that hadn't experienced life yet. A few still looked like boys, not men. I prayed my words would sink deep into their soul and make them see this was not a wise decision. They were following Peter down a deathly trail.

"You don't have to…" I started to say again as Peter interrupted.

"If you don't want to go, you better say something now, or else," Peter snidely commented.

"Why are you following him?" I asked. "Yes, Peter, you are a great leader and I see you are going to do some great things in the future, but this," I stopped and pleaded directly to Peter, "this isn't one of them."

"I have to do this, Mary," Peter responded with a matter-of-fact tone. "Okay, everyone knows what they are doing, so it's time to head out."

"Should we pray first?"

Chapter 72
Thomas

"Should we pray first?" I asked, looking around the room and feeling the weight on all of our shoulders. "I mean, I think Jesus would have wanted us to pray before we separated."

"Fine," Peter snorted as he said a quick prayer for protection and strength to defeat the enemy.

"That's it?" I asked amazed. "We are about to go out there and that's the prayer? To ask God to give us success and skill and to keep our bodies from growing weak?"

"If you think you can do any better, pray as you walk," Peter said disgruntled. "We have to leave now and get in our places before it's too late."

The eight of us started to make our way to the door. I patted John and Mary on the shoulder as I passed. John looked up at me hurt and Mary was still crying, but I couldn't stay with them. That wasn't going to solve anything.

I left the room with John and Mary still bound to their chairs as Simon stood by the window to watch each of us depart and go our separate directions. We quietly went down the steps as a group like we had three nights ago. Then, we had exited the home singing a psalm of praise, but this morning there wasn't a song to be sung. The deathly silence was our anthem.

As we left in separate directions, we didn't talk; there were no tearful goodbyes or emotional good lucks. There were no words at all.

It was as if each of us knew we were making a mistake. A deadly mistake.

Peter, Andrew, and I walked quickly toward the tomb. My heart was pounding in anticipation of what was going to be happening soon. I thought Peter would say something, to tell us more of his plan, but he never said a word. He walked transfixed with his goal in sight, while I walked with a different plan in mind. Andrew and Peter were slightly ahead of me when I saw an alley to my right. No one said anything, and I didn't think they would realize I wasn't with them until they were further down the road.

They passed the alley and I darted into the shaded entryway, hiding behind a barrel. I waited a few minutes to see if they would come back looking for me, but they never did. I never heard them say my name. Peter had a focused mind.

I quickly left the alleyway and ran back to the place we had just left. I weaved in and out of the streets, but I never saw anyone. I wondered if I should be frightened of being caught, but I was more fearful of what was going to happen.

I made my last turn and saw a woman slowly heading my way. I slowed my pace and was about to pass her as I saw her hands were full, and a jar was about to fall out of her hands.

I quickly grabbed the loose jar and put it in the cleft of her elbow as she started to weep. My nostrils inhaled the contents of the jars, and I instinctively looked up. Her wet eyes caught my heart.

"Thomas, is that you?"

Chapter 73

Mary

"Thomas, is that you?" I asked, shocked to see his face so early in the morning.

"Mary, it's not safe," Thomas warned me as he probably knew where I was heading. The jars were filled with oils and ointments to finish the burial process of my son. "Turn around and go back home."

"I can't," I cried. "I need to see him."

"Mary, please, you are making a mistake going to the tomb right now. Please wait a little while longer and then some of us will go there with you. But right now," he said looking at the twilight sky, "right now it is too dangerous."

I looked at him confused. "How is it dangerous?" I asked looking up and down the road. "You are the only person I have seen so far."

"Just trust me, Mary," Thomas pleaded once again. "Just trust me." He leaned in and hugged me deeply. I needed to feel that hug. I had tried to sleep through the night, but I could only toss and turn. I had told a few of the ladies to meet me at the grave at sunrise so we could start the preparations. It took me some time at home to gather all the jars because my emotions kept overtaking me.

A mother should never have to bury her child. Never.

"But I'm supposed to meet the others there," I said, still confused at Thomas' plea. "I don't understand."

"Go to their homes, Mary," I pleaded one more time before I turned away. "Just don't go to the tomb."

Chapter 74
Thomas

"Just don't go to the tomb," I said before taking off again. I knew if she didn't listen to me, there was going to be much more trouble. Peter was going to try to kill the guard. Mary was going to be at the tomb with some of her friends. That combination of events wasn't going to end well for anyone.

Mary didn't need to see Peter's vengeance first-hand. She had already been through so much. Seeing Peter kill would probably push her over the edge. She was like a mother to all of us. Seeing one son die was something I could not comprehend, but seeing another son take a life was much worse. Peter wasn't going to kill in self-defense. He was going to do so with anger and revenge.

I ran down the last alleyway making it back to the home. As I ran through the secret passageway to the stairs, I heard something strange. I heard four voices. Not three.

I quietly tiptoed up the stairs. I didn't want my cover to be blown. I wanted to rescue Mary and John so the three of us could try to stop what was going to happen. I didn't know how we were going to do it, but I knew we were going to have to try to save everyone's life.

"What are you doing here?" I heard Simon ask, a little rattled.

"Peter wanted me to come and tell you to go join the others," the strange voice said.

"Which one?" Simon asked startled. "I thought I was supposed to stay and watch over Mary and John."

"Change of plans," the voice said.

I heard a pair of footsteps heading my way from the upper room, and I quickly darted down the few steps I had taken and hid behind a stack of baskets. I pressed my body against the wall and waited for Simon to exit the stairs and leave the alleyway.

He slowly made his way down and then left as commanded.

I didn't know what to do. I weighed the pros and cons because I thought I could have taken Simon if he tried to stop me, but I didn't know who was up there.

Andrew, I thought. They must have figured out what I was doing and sent Andrew back. He was slightly larger than Simon and had the strength and stamina of a fisherman. I didn't think I could take him, but I knew I couldn't wait down here. Sitting here wasn't going to do anything.

I peered around the corner to see up the stairs, but no one was on them. I quietly walked up the steps until I was on the top one. I took in a deep breath and made up my mind.

I barged into the room and saw James tightening the knots on Mary's bindings.

"Look out!" Mary screamed at the top of her lungs.

"Stop that!" I screamed running in James' direction and throwing all my body weight on top of him. We tumbled back onto the hard floor. "Let them go!"

"Thomas," James said as I started to punch his stomach as many times as I could, hoping I could subdue him and then free the others.

"Thomas, stop!" John yelled from behind. "He was helping us."

I stopped with my right fist about to slam into James' side. "What?" I said, looking behind as John already had one hand free and was starting to loosen the other knots.

"That's what I was trying to say," James said with a shaky breath. "I'm here to help."

"So am I," I said getting off of James and helping him to his feet. I quickly went over and started to untie Mary's knots.

"I thought you were siding with Peter," Mary said apprehensively.

"After they tied you two up, I thought it was stupid to tell them I was on your side," I answered grabbing my knife from my waist and cutting the knots. "When I was tying you up, I tried to let you know I was going to come back, but you never looked me in the eyes. I was going to wink at you, but you kept looking away from me."

"I was hurt," Mary said painfully. "I'd thought you were on our side."

"We all need to be on one side," I said plainly. "Peter can't see it yet, and I'm afraid he's not going to until it's too late. We are stronger together than divided," I said as I helped Mary to her feet.

"So, did Peter really ask you to come back here?" John asked James as he was untying his feet.

"No," James smiled. "I had been listening from the street all night. When everyone was asleep I thought I could come up here and get you two out, but I didn't want to risk it."

I looked around the room, and the four of us were all free and ready to make our move.

"Let's go stop Peter."

Chapter 75

John

"Let's go stop Peter," I said as the four of us ran down the steps. My heart was racing with hope that it wasn't too late to change the course that could abruptly end the lives of all my friends. I understood Peter's frustration and pain, since I wanted to smother him hours after Jesus died. But killing wasn't the answer. It wouldn't solve anything.

There would always be someone else to blame for this, even after we killed all the Roman guards. Next we would have to go after all the townspeople who had cheered for Jesus to be crucified. It was going to be a never-ending act of retaliation.

The four of us started to run down the road when I burst out ahead of everyone. We were not afraid of being seen anymore. We wanted to be seen. We wanted all this to stop.

I turned down a road toward the tomb. We were about ten minutes away when I heard a voice from behind.

"John?" the voice said, but I didn't stop. I had a destination to reach. I hoped it would end there, but I knew that was too hopeful in thinking. Even if we got to Peter, we still had a battle with him and the others.

"Mary?" the voice said again but from a distance.

"We have to stop Peter!" Mary shouted as she continued to run. Then I heard another pair of feet running with us. I knew I shouldn't look back, but I needed to know what was going on.

I looked, and in the distance, running as a group, were James, Mary, Thomas, and Thaddaeus. I smiled, seeing Thaddaeus running with us, not against us. Our group had grown to five. We might have a chance.

I continued to run at full speed as the group behind me started to fall behind. Being the youngest sometimes had its advantages. I turned down another road and sprinted past a woman with her hands full. I didn't look. I just kept running.

"John?" the woman shouted, but I didn't care who she was. I had one thing on my mind and it was to stop Peter.

I looked ahead and saw that in the far off horizon, the sun was starting to rise. A sliver of light was starting to come my way as if showing me a path to run toward. And I kept running.

I rounded the last turn and knew the tomb was a straight shot up the gravel road. I started to slow my pace because I didn't want to be heard. I squinted my eyes, and I could vaguely see two men crouching about fifty cubits from the tomb, behind a couple of bushes.

I stopped and hid behind a tree. I looked back but didn't see anyone else yet. My speed was one of my best assets. I was always running errands, not because I was the youngest, I told myself, but because I was the fastest.

Once again, I turned my attention to Andrew and Peter who were intently watching the two guards in front of the tomb. I could tell Peter was talking to Andrew, using his hands as he spoke. I wished I could hear him.

I swallowed my fear and started to move a little closer. The sun continued to rise, shining more light on the wet ground. It had rained most of the last two days with very little sunlight shining through the clouds.

Suddenly, Peter snuck away from Andrew. I lost him in the bushes that lined the path to the tomb, and I knew he was making his move.

It was time to make mine.

I looked behind me, and in the distance I saw my friends who were slowly jogging my direction. I jumped up but stayed hidden behind another bush to warn them of Andrew who was hiding a short distance away.

I saw James nod as I pointed towards where I thought Peter had crawled. He took my hint and started to walk in that direction. I knew I needed to make my move now so James could stop Peter.

I tiptoed across the road and snuck up behind Andrew who didn't see me coming. I wrapped my hands around his neck and covered his mouth.

"Don't say a word," I said to him as he tried to fight me off, but I had the advantage for once. I had the surprise attack. He tried to buck me off his back, but I didn't let up. He started rolling around on the ground, slamming me into the mud, but my grip was firmly planted over his mouth. "This is a bad idea!" I ranted in his ear. "Do you want to die?"

He stopped fighting.

But I didn't know for how long.

Mary and Thaddaeus showed up beside us as I continued to keep Andrew's mouth sealed with my hand.

"Where did Peter go?" I asked.

He didn't answer. He just closed his eyes and pretended like he didn't hear me.

"Come on, Andrew," Thaddaeus said, "you know this isn't right."

My ears perked up. It was one thing to know someone agreed with you, but it was another thing to hear them actually say it. I hoped that Thaddaeus' words would sink through to Andrew.

"Is he going to do it here?" Thomas asked. "Because Mary is on her way. Do you want her to see this?"

Andrew's eyes looked mournful at Thomas' mention of Mary.

"You know, Andrew," Thomas said. "You know this isn't Peter."

Chapter 76
Thomas

"You know this isn't Peter," I said, hoping he realized that. "He is angry and hurt like all of us. He is grieving in his own way, but that doesn't make it right." I stopped and looked at the group around us. They nodded in agreement. "I am breaking inside over Jesus' death, and I want them to pay too, but at the same time, I know Jesus wouldn't want it this way."

"No," Mary chimed in. "He wouldn't want to see us all like this."

"We are no different than the rest of the world if we do this," John agreed. "Years later some of the world would agree this was right to kill, but what would your family think?"

"What would Jesus think?" Thaddaeus asked solemnly. "I don't think he would be very proud of us if we followed through with this."

Tears started to fill Andrew's eyes. I didn't know if it was the thought of Jesus not being around, or that we were bullying him, or if his heart was changing. I didn't know, but I felt he needed to be free. I looked at John to remove his hand from Andrew's lips.

"Are you sure?" John tentatively asked, but he finally removed his hand.

Andrew looked around us all and wiped away his tears. He took a deep breath and looked into my eyes. "I'm sorry," he said as he looked at each one of us. "I'm so sorry."

"There's nothing to be sorry about," I said, patting my friend on his shoulder. "We are in this together."

"Really?" Andrew said cynically. "We are in this together? Want to tell Peter that?"

"We are," Thaddaeus said optimistically. "After what we have been through the last few days, anyone would go a little crazy and say things they would never say in a normal situation. We have all said things we regret."

"Like what?" Andrew asked as he sniffled.

"I started to doubt if Jesus was anything special," I said sadly, looking around the huddle of friends and wondering if they had ever thought that.

Sadly, each of them nodded their heads.

"We have all thought these thoughts," Mary said.

"Well, that's going to make this hard," Andrew said as he took a deep breath. "Peter!" he yelled at the top of his lungs.

John quickly tackled Andrew and buried his face into the ground muffling his screams. He continued to try to yell a warning, but all he got was a mouthful of mud each time.

"Why?"

Chapter 77

Mary Magdalene

"Why?" I asked with a broken heart as my lips quivered in pain. I watched as the three men held Andrew down and knew I had to make my way toward the tomb.

I looked ahead and could faintly see the two soldiers. I looked back, and in the distance I saw an aging woman with her arms full and her heart empty. I scanned the horizon behind the bush and noticed something moving in the garden beside the tomb.

"Peter," I said softly to myself as I stood up. But my legs started to shake. Then my entire being shook from head to toe. "You can do this!" I told myself, but by the looks on their faces, I realized it wasn't me shaking. It was the earth.

The shaking continued to rattle all of us as John slid off Andrew's back and Thaddaeus and Thomas also let go of their grip. Andrew looked terrified and jumped up, running away from the tomb, back into the city.

"Go after him," I commanded Thomas and Thaddaeus. They shakily got up and ran after him.

I looked back up at the garden and saw Peter standing up and moving toward the tomb.

I looked ahead of me and saw one of the guards running in our direction. I quickly forced John back down as we cowered behind the bush. The Roman guard rushed past us at a great speed. Even if we were not hiding, I don't know if he would have noticed us.

"He's going after him!" I shouted to John as we immediately got up and started running to the tomb.

John quickly darted out ahead of me, but I was trying to run as fast as I could. I watched as Peter ran through the garden and headed toward the tomb, watching the stunned guard with vengeful eyes. Peter was ready for battle with his sword out as the guard stood stupefied.

John reached the guard first and got between him and Peter. "Peter, you don't have to do this!"

"Get out of my way, John!" Peter shouted venomously.

"Stop!" I screamed, making my way to the scene. I looked at Peter as he clenched his teeth, ready to slice the guard with his sword. I looked at John as he bravely stayed calm, trying to coach Peter down from the proverbial cliff he was about to throw himself off of. I looked at the guard who stared dumbfounded at the commotion. He didn't even have his sword drawn. He didn't look like he was ready for a fight. He looked shocked and confused.

I got closer and noticed I knew the guard.

"Longinus?" I said as Peter and John both looked at me in shock.

"You know him?" Peter asked in unrelenting rage. "You know the guard who killed Jesus? You know him by name?"

"It's not like that," I cried watching my tragedies over the last few days swirl into a foggy mess. "He saved my life two nights ago!"

"He did what?" John asked in shock.

"He's…" Longinus started to say, but he couldn't get the words out. He just looked dazed and started to ramble.

"Peter, just drop your sword," I pleaded. "He's a good man. He saved me."

"Saved you from what?" Peter asked in doubt. "What did this killer save you from?"

"Barabbas," I feebly said, not wanting to think back to that night but unable to help it. "When I left you all two nights ago and I was walking home, Barabbas attacked me. He was going to rape and kill me. He said so." I started crying as I relived the horrific moments that seemed like years ago but had been less than 48 hours. "He was telling me what he was going to do to me and then I heard something so I kicked him and screamed. He saved me."

"But he killed Jesus!" Peter yelled, gripping his sword tighter with both hands. "He killed Jesus," he said again.

"If he didn't do it, someone else would have," I said painstakingly. "He didn't know what he was doing, Peter. But you do know."

"It's not fair!" Peter groaned in agony, holding his sword up to attack as John was also begging Peter to drop it.

"I can't now," Peter said. "He knows who I am and he will come after me."

"He's gone," Longinus finally said, waking up to the commotion around him.

I finally understood what Longinus was talking about. I looked behind the three men and noticed the tomb was open.

"He's gone."

Chapter 78

Longinus

"He's gone," I said amazed. Atticus took off running the moment after the earthquake when he noticed the tomb was opened and the grave was empty.

"They are going to kill us!" Atticus ranted in a fit of self-preservation. "We had one job to do and it was to guard the tomb, and now the tomb is open and it's empty. They are going to say we failed and we will be blamed and killed! Run Longinus! Run!" he'd screamed as he took off from the tomb. But my legs couldn't run. I was frozen to the scene.

"Where's the body?" Peter asked, lifting the sword to slice my throat. In any other situation, I would have quickly reacted, either wounding or killing him, but I didn't want to do either. I wanted to find out what happened as well.

"I don't know," I said sincerely. "I've been here all night and no one has gotten by. Then the quake happened and the tomb opened and now the body is gone. It doesn't make any sense."

"No it doesn't!" Peter hissed. "What did you do? Did you hide it so we couldn't properly bury it? Did you move it somewhere else as a sick joke? Tell me, what did you do with Jesus?"

What did I do? I wondered as I flashed to two days ago. I was cruel and vicious; heartless and vile; evil and sadistic; criminal and merciless. I was obeying orders.

I had heard his shoulder socket pop out of place as Cassius had pulled on his arm for me to hammer the spike through his wrist. There were some sounds that one didn't hear often, and the sound of bone separating used to always give me a feeling that nothing else could. He'd groaned in pain with each slamming of the hammer as I made sure to hit the nerve that inflicted the most pain. Blood had spurted out, even though I didn't know where it was coming from since we had already beaten him bloody.

I'd grabbed his trembling legs and placed his feet on top of one another and drove the spike through both of them until the nail hit the wood. Then I continued to hammer for good measure.

I had stood and looked at the sprawled man, spitting on his face before I disrobed him so his nakedness could be seen by all. I had helped raise the cross and watched as his eyes bulged out in pain as the beam fell into the perfectly dug hole, causing a sudden jolting pain from the impact.

I had stood under him and asked him a few questions. They were cruel questions, but that was my job: to be an executioner. I wasn't there to make friends. I wasn't there to be sympathetic. I was there to act out the decrees issued. And his decree was death.

I remembered standing with Cassius and Maximus, looking at the three dying men, making bets on who was going to last the longest. That was our game. The winner didn't have to do much to take down the bodies. Maximus won that day as he said Jesus would be the first one to die.

"What did I do?" I stammered as tears began to trickle down my cheeks. "I have done more horrible things in one day than you have done in your entire lives. But the one thing I haven't done," I said looking at the four of them, "was take your friend."

"If you didn't, who did?" Peter shouted.

"The tomb has been closed; no one has been around here," I said, but then I couldn't be sure. "I have only been guarding the tomb since dusk, but I don't think anyone else would have taken the body."

"Are you sure about that?" Mary cried. "Who would do a thing like this?"

"I don't know," I said. "All I do know is, I didn't do it."

Peter kept the sword up to my throat and I stepped closer. The young boy left us and walked into the tomb. "I deserve death," I said feeling the blade on my throat. "I deserve this."

"You killed my friend."

Chapter 79

Peter

"You killed my friend," I said pressing the blade to his throat. If I moved my hand slightly, he would be dead.

"Friends, you need to see this!" John shouted from the tomb.

"You killed my friend!" I said again, looking into Longinus' eyes. He had the look of a Roman guard. His handsome face and blond hair, his chiseled biceps and calves showcased his prowess. I looked into his eyes and saw another soldier from the other night.

We had all just crossed the brook of Kidron and entered into the garden of Gethsemane after the Passover meal. All but Judas Iscariot. Soldiers and priests surrounded us with torches and weapons, ready to attack if we made a move.

"Whom do you seek?" Jesus had asked.

"Jesus of Nazareth," one of the guards answered.

"I am he," Jesus calmly replied. "So, if you seek me, let these men go."

I had grabbed my sword and struck the high priest's servant, cutting off his right ear. I thought Jesus was going to run or fight or do something, but all he'd said was, "Put your sword into its sheath; shall I not drink the cup that the Father has given me?"

"Put your sword into its sheath," said a familiar voice.

"Who said that?"

"Said what?" Mary cried, kneeling on the ground.

"Who said, 'Put your sword into its sheath'?" I asked Mary and the guard as James approached from the garden.

"No one said anything," James said.

I lowered my sword from the guard's throat and put it away. I looked into the tomb and it was empty. I poked my head in, unsure if I should go into Jesus' tomb. I felt like I was trespassing on someone else's property, like I was invading a sacred space. I closed my eyes and an aroma of the oils and ointments they put on Jesus two nights ago was still strong. I stepped into the tomb and found John standing beside the table that had held Jesus, but all that remained was a neatly folded linen.

"Why did they take the time to fold it?" John asked.

"I… I…" I stammered because I didn't understand what was going on. I didn't know how things could be worse, but they kept falling more and more apart. "I don't know."

I walked out of the empty tomb feeling just as bare. Mary tried to say something to me, but I didn't pay attention. I was shocked.

I had come to act out revenge. But now, I was left unsure of everything. I stopped and stared at the rock that was in front of the tomb and tried to move it. One person couldn't move it; it would take a few strong men to move something like this, especially with muddy ground where people's feet couldn't get good traction.

"Where did they take him?"

Chapter 80

Mary Magdalene

"Where did they take him?" I asked as Peter walked by, but he just shook his head. Slowly, John came out of the tomb and I asked him the same question, but he just stared at me with distant eyes as he, too, walked away.

I looked at Longinus and he looked as alone as I felt.

"I don't understand this," he said, scratching his head and looking at the stone and then in all directions as if trying to figure out how someone could have done it.

"Mary," someone said behind me as I watched Jesus' mother walk closer to the tomb. "Did you come to help with the body?"

I started to cry. I didn't know how to respond to such a sincere gesture to come and prepare her son's body for burial.

"He's not here, Mary," I said feebly.

"What?" Mary asked. "It sounded like you said, 'he's not here.'"

"He's gone," I said rushing to her and hugging her. "He's gone."

"I don't believe you," Mary said as she grabbed my hand pulling me toward the tomb as Longinus followed. Mary and I were crying as Longinus stood close by. He paced around the tomb as we stood motionless.

"My baby," Mary cried as she touched the linen on the table. "Where have they taken him?"

Suddenly, a bright light shone within the tomb. It was brighter than the sun and there before us stood two men. One said, "Woman, why are you weeping?"

"They have taken away my Lord, and I do not know where they have laid him."

"Do not be alarmed. You seek Jesus of Nazareth, who was crucified. He has risen; he is not here. See the place where they laid him. But go, tell his disciples and Peter that he is going before you to Galilee. There you will see him, just as he told you."

Suddenly, the light faded and the three of us were left alone in the tomb.

Mary immediately left, rejoicing as she walked away from the tomb. I could hear her singing as she walked back towards the city.

Longinus and I stood in silence.

"What just happened?" he asked in confusion. "Did you see that, or am I dreaming?"

I looked over at him. "You're not dreaming."

"So what was that?" he asked as fear surged through his body, causing him to turn white.

"Come on," I said pulling him out of the tomb. "Sit here and take a few breaths." I walked away into the garden and sat down and wept.

"Woman, why are you weeping? Whom are you seeking?" a man said to me.

"Sir, if you have carried him away, tell me where you have laid him, and I will take him away."

"Mary."

I turned to the man and suddenly my eyes could see Him in all His glory. "Rabboni!" I cried. It was Jesus! He was standing here in front of me. My heart fluttered. My pulse raced. I felt a joy that I had never experienced in my life. I went to hug Him, but He stopped me.

"Do not cling to Me, for I have not yet ascended to the Father; but go to My brothers and say to them, 'I am ascending to my Father and your Father, to My God and your God,'" Jesus said and immediately disappeared.

"Longinus!" I screamed causing him to run up the garden.

"What? What's wrong?" he asked out of breath from the quick sprint. "What, Mary?"

I started crying tears of joy. I had a smile on my face that no tears could wash away.

"Mary, what happened?" he asked again, looking at me confused.

I looked at him and exploded in jubilation. I gave him the biggest hug I had ever given. "He's alive, Longinus! He is really alive! I just saw Him. Those people, that light in the tomb, that wasn't a dream. I saw it too! Those were angels! Jesus isn't in the tomb because He has risen from the dead! He is alive!"

"How can that be?" Longinus asked. "I, I killed him," he said solemnly. "I pierced his side and made sure he was dead. I took down his dead body. How is he alive? It doesn't make sense."

"I promise you, what you saw, no one will believe, but you have to tell it! You have to!" I squirmed with excitement. "So, do you believe what you saw?"

He stood for a moment and looked at me. Then he looked back at the empty tomb with the stone rolled away from the entrance. He glanced up at the sunny sky that had been gloomy the last two days. He squinted his piercing eyes toward Golgotha, the place where he'd executed Jesus. He then circled back to me.

"So, do you believe?" I asked once again.

272

He rubbed his chin as he thought deeply.

"Come with me," I said with a warm, inviting smile. We walked down the garden and I started to tell him everything I could of Jesus. His miracles, His teachings, His kindness. We walked the early morning streets with the sun steadily rising behind us, warming our backs from the last two days of shadows and rain. I felt like the fog I had been living in the last two days had been lifted. The nightmare had ended. I still didn't understand it all, but I knew this wasn't the end. I knew, in a way, this was the start of a brand new beginning.

We made it back to the place where we had been meeting the last two days. The home looked different. It wasn't a sad, decrepit building I had visualized it to be in the last two days. It was warm and friendly, with a welcoming feeling at its secret entrance. I was about to step into the alleyway and go to the upper room when I stopped. I turned and looked Longinus in his piercing eyes, remembering two nights earlier when he'd saved my life.

We had been in this similar situation after he'd walked me back to Mary's.

"Stay safe. My name is Longinus, by the way," he'd said under the darkened sky.

"Pleased to meet you, Longinus. My name is Mary. And if you ever need anything, just let me know."

My memory ended and I came back to the present with Longinus looking at me questioningly.

"Two nights ago, you said to let you know if I ever needed anything," he said timidly.

"Yes," I said with a strange sensation running down my spine, as if all the moving pieces were aligning perfectly.

"I think I want to know more about this Jesus," he said with a grin. "I think I want to know a lot more about him."

"Come," I said with me a gentle smile as I reached out my hand. "Follow me."